Munmun

OrangeBooks Publication

1st Floor, Rajhans Arcade, Mall Road, Kohka, Bhilai, Chhattisgarh 490020

Website: **www.orangebooks.in**

© Copyright, 2025, Author

All rights reserved. No part of this book may be reproduced, stored in a retrieval system, or transmitted, in any form by any means, electronic, mechanical, magnetic, optical, chemical, manual, photocopying, recording or otherwise, without the prior written consent of its writer.

First Edition, 2025

ISBN: 978-93-6554-800-6

Price: Rs. 242.00

The opinions/ contents expressed in this book are solely of the author and do not represent the opinions/ standings/ thoughts of OrangeBooks.

Printed in India

Munmun

More than a mere Crush

Deepak Kumar

OrangeBooks Publication
www.orangebooks.in

This Book is dedicated to my
"Chhoti Ungli Wali".

I will always be thankful to you for making me feel special

I wish I could name you, but believe me,
You are the sweetest addiction I would never want to recover from.

About the Author

Deepak Kumar, a native of Patna, Bihar, has always been drawn to the world of words. His journey with literature began early, fuelled by a deep curiosity and an undying love for storytelling. Growing up in the historic city of Patna, he completed his schooling there before pursuing his higher education at the prestigious Patna College, Patna University, where Literature became his core subject.

Currently working as a Stenographer at the Accountant General Office, Patna, Deepak has never let his passion for writing take a backseat. Having spent years reading and absorbing the essence of countless literary works, he finally took the leap into authorship.

Munmun, More Than a mere Crush is his debut book—a heartfelt tale that blends youthful emotions, personal growth, and the bittersweet nostalgia of first love. Through this book, he brings forth a story that many can relate to, yet few dare to express.

With this book, Deepak not only fulfils a long-held dream but also takes his first step toward a future filled with storytelling.

Disclaimer

This book is a work of fiction. Any resemblance to actual persons, living or dead, or to real events, places, or incidents is purely coincidental. The characters, settings, and situations in this story are products of the author's imagination and are not intended to depict or reference any real individuals or occurrences.

The views and opinions expressed in this book are solely those of the author and do not reflect the beliefs or perspectives of any individual, group, or organization. This story is meant for entertainment and emotional connection, and it should be read as a fictional narrative rather than a reflection of reality.

Thank you for being a part of this journey. Happy reading!

Munmun
"More than a mere Crush"
Written by
Deepak Kumar

A Note from the Author

Writing this book has been a journey—one that started as a simple story but soon turned into an emotional rollercoaster of memories, realizations, and lessons. This is not just Romii's story. It is a reflection of many young hearts who have experienced their first crush, their first heartbreak, and the difficult yet necessary transition from emotions to ambitions.

Through Romii, I wanted to capture the innocence of young love, the confusion of growing up, and the struggle of balancing emotions with responsibilities. We all have a "Munmun" in our lives—someone who once made our world brighter, someone who unknowingly taught us some of the most valuable lessons. But the real question is—do we hold on to the past, or do we use it as fuel to move forward?

If this book has taught you anything, I hope it's this: Love is beautiful, but self-growth is essential. It's okay to feel deeply, to be lost in emotions, to cherish memories—but never at the cost of your own dreams and ambitions.

To every student, every youngster reading this—your emotions are valid, but so is your future. Life will always give you choices. Choose wisely.

And to Romii—wherever he exists in the real world—I hope you know that your story has touched many hearts.

With gratitude,
Deepak Kumar

Acknowledgment

First of all, a huge shukriya to all my dear readers, for tolerating me for at least two hours while reading this book. I know, I know—many of you might have thought, "Bhai, yeh kya likh raha hai!" But still, you started reading this book, which means either you connected with Romii's journey or you were just too stubborn to leave a book unfinished. Either way, dil se thank you!

If you liked the book (or even if you didn't but still have something to say), I am most active on Instagram (@deepakkumarsrivastav2805)—so feel free to message me, comment, or drop a review there. Your feedback will mean the world to me!

A special thanks to my dear friend for creating such an attractive cover page. Bhai, You are the best!

To my family and friends, who stood by me through thick and thin—you all are my biggest strength. Without your support, this book wouldn't have been possible.

And last but not least, a very polite and heartfelt thank you to Munmun—for unknowingly making me an author. Some people come into your life as a lesson, some as a blessing—she was both.

With appreciation and warmth
Deepak Kumar

"There was a time when her smile was my universe.

And today, I smile knowing that once,

I was a part of hers."

Prologue

Echoes by the Ganges

The evening breeze carried the scent of the river, a mix of damp earth and nostalgia, as Romii sat on the old stone steps of Patna College, staring at the slow-moving waters of the Ganges. The sky above him was painted in hues of orange and pink, the kind of sunset that made the city pause for a moment. But Romii wasn't looking at the sky. His eyes were fixed on the ripples in the water—small, delicate waves that formed, grew, and eventually faded into nothing.

Just like memories, he thought.

It had been years since those days—since she was a part of his life. Yet, even today, as he sat here alone, he could hear echoes of the past in his mind. Munmun. Her name was still a whisper in his heart, like an old song that never really leaves you.

The city had changed. The roads were more crowded, the college looked older, and life had moved on. And so had he. Or at least, that's what he told himself.

Romii took out his phone and scrolled through his contacts. He had deleted her number long ago, but the habit of looking for it had never really left. Funny, he thought, how we hold on to things that no longer exist.

For a fleeting moment, he wondered—where would she be now? Was she happy? Did she ever think about him? Or was he just another forgotten page in the book of her life?

A gust of wind made the water shimmer under the fading sunlight, and just like that, he let his thoughts drift back to where it all began.

To the boy he once was.

To the college he never wanted to join.

To the first time he saw her again after school.

To the lame jokes he cracked just to see her smile.

To the night when he cried alone, holding his phone, waiting for a message that never came.

And before he knew it, time rewound itself, pulling him into the past.

The Ganges kept flowing, just like life, carrying both forgotten and unforgettable stories with it.

And Romii? He was about to tell his.

Because some stories don't fade away with time.

Some stay. Forever

Content

Chapter 1: The Beginning..1

Chapter 2: The Topper's Nature 7

Chapter 3: First Meet with Munmun 13

Chapter 4: The Talking Stage 19

Chapter 5: Shaima..24

Chapter 6: A Word from Shaima..28

Chapter 7: The Smiling Ride..33

Chapter 8: Old is Gold 39

Chapter 9: The Confession...45

Chapter 10: The Confusion and the Future Goals................51

Chapter 11: The Caste Issue...57

Chapter 12: The Mental Blockage..63

Chapter 13: The Situationship 69

Chapter 14: The Worst Day..75

Chapter 15: A Word from Munmun's Father.........................81

Chapter 16: A Word from Munmun's Mother.......................86

Chapter 17: The Sleepless Nights 93

Chapter 18: A Word from Romii's Mother............................99

Chapter 19: The Realisation 103

Chapter 20: Career Comes First 107

Chapter 21: Rewind to the Past 111

Chapter 22: A Message for the Youngsters 116

Chapter 23: A Word from Avikal and Amit 122

Chapter 24: Shaima Again 126

Chapter 25: A Word from Romii's First Crush, Munmun 128

Chapter 1: The Beginning

My name is Romi.

People often ask, "What's your full name?" but I've learned to avoid that question. Not because I don't like my name, but because it's unnecessarily long. So long that by the time a teacher finished calling it out during attendance, half the class had already lost interest in the subject.

But let's not get distracted.

This story begins in the summer of 2016, a summer so hot that even the air felt like it was straight out of a tandoor. The kind of summer where stepping outside meant becoming a roasted version of yourself. The roads in Patna shimmered in the heat, autos refused to go by the meter (because apparently, the sun was charging them extra), and shopkeepers wiped sweat off their faces while yelling at kids not to touch the cold drink bottles.

And in the middle of all this, there was me—sitting in my cramped little room, staring at my computer screen, waiting for my matriculation results.

This wasn't just any result. This was THE RESULT. The one that decided everything—college, career, and how much respect I'd get from nosy neighbours like Sharma Ji, who was always lurking around, waiting for an opportunity to compare me with his son, Bunty.

I took a deep breath and typed in my roll number.

The website took forever to load. My heart was pounding like a drum at a baraat. My palms were sweating. My mind raced with thoughts.

"What if I score 10 CGPA?"

I could already imagine the scene—my mother hugging me, my father giving me an approving nod, my relatives calling one after another to congratulate me. Maybe even the school principal would mention my name in the morning assembly.

The page loaded.

9.4 CGPA.

For a second, I just stared at the screen. Maybe there was a glitch? Maybe if I refreshed the page, it would change to 10?

I refreshed. 9.4.

I refreshed again. Still 9.4.

Reality hit me like a truck.

It wasn't a bad score. It was actually pretty decent. But the problem was, in my house, "decent" was never enough.

I turned to my father, who was sitting on the chair behind me. He looked at the screen. Then he looked at me. His face remained expressionless, but I knew exactly what he was thinking.

"Bas itna hi?"

That was all he said. Just three words. No shouting, no anger—just disappointment so deep that it cut through me like a knife.

I had seen that look before—when our washing machine broke down, when the neighbour's dog peed on our doormat, when our electricity bill was higher than expected. That was the look he was giving me now.

My mother, sensing the tension, quickly tried to fix things.

"9.4 is also very good," she said, patting my shoulder. But even she sounded unsure.

I forced a smile, but inside, I was sinking

And then, like a villain entering at the worst possible moment, came Sharma Ji.

This man had no business being in our house, yet he somehow always appeared during important family discussions—especially when they involved my failures.

He peeked inside. "Result aa gaya?" (Did the result come?)

Before I could answer, my father spoke. "Haan, bas 9.4."

Sharma Ji's face lit up. "Arre koi baat nahi. Dekhna, humara Bunty aage nikal jayega." (No worries. Our Bunty will soon overtake him.)

Bunty.

A boy who could barely spell his own name without making a mistake. A boy whose greatest achievement in life was winning a boondi-eating competition at his cousin's wedding.

I wanted to scream.

But instead, I just nodded, forcing another fake smile.

As soon as Sharma Ji left, my father stood up and walked away without another word. That was worse than any scolding.

I sat back down and stared at the screen again. 9.4. The number felt like a slap on my face.

But the nightmare was only beginning.

The College Disaster

I had always imagined myself studying in one of the best colleges in Patna—Science College, BN College, Patna College. I had spent years believing I was meant for bigger things.

But one by one, the doors shut on my face.

With my 9.4 CGPA, I wasn't eligible for Science College. BN College was already full. Patna College had cut-offs that made me feel like an average student for the first time in my life.

And then, there was only one option left.

Bal Dayal College.

Now, let me tell you something about Bal Dayal College.

If good colleges were five-star hotels, Bal Dayal was a roadside dhaba with broken chairs and an expired menu.

It wasn't a place where students chose to go—it was a place where they ended up.

No entrance exams. No cut-offs. No interviews. Just pay the fees and congratulations—you were now a student of Bal Dayal College!

When I told my father, he didn't say a word. He just gave me a long look and sighed. That sigh carried the weight of a thousand disappointments.

I sat in front of the admission form, my pen hovering over the paper.

I didn't belong here. I knew it. My heart screamed, "No! This is not your future!"

But what could I do? Fate had other plans.

And so, with a heavy heart and a mind full of self-doubt, I signed the form.

I was officially a student of Bal Dayal College.

It felt like the end of everything I had dreamed of.

But what I didn't know was that this so-called "B-grade" college was about to introduce me to someone who would change my life forever.

Her name was Munmun.

And this was just the beginning.

Question for the readers

1. Do you ever feel the pressure to always be the best, just so you don't get left behind? If yes, Are you tackling this pressure or just ignoring it?

2. Do you not think that your life is shaped by Society's choices and not by yours?

Chapter 2: The Topper's Nature

People always assume that toppers are born with some magical power that makes them smarter than everyone else. That they don't have to work hard, that they wake up in the morning and automatically know all the answers.

Well, let me tell you the truth.

There was nothing magical about me.

I wasn't born a topper. I became one because I refused to be left behind.

From the moment I understood competition, I knew one thing—I had to be ahead of everyone. Not because I wanted fame or because I loved studying, but because I had seen what life looked like for those who were left behind. And I did not want that life.

Meet My Family

I come from a middle-class family in Patna, where every rupee is spent carefully, and dreams are measured in terms of affordability. My father works as a waiter at Hotel Samridhi International—one of the well-known hotels in the city. He wears a white uniform with a red tie, takes orders from rich guests, and serves food that we could never afford to eat ourselves.

He never complains, never talks about how tiring his job is. But sometimes, when he comes home late at night, I see him sitting quietly on the balcony, rubbing his sore feet. That silence speaks louder than any words.

My mother is a housewife, which means she works all day but never gets paid for it. She wakes up before the sun, cooks, cleans, washes clothes, and makes sure everything in the house is running smoothly. And in between all this, she still finds time to worry about me.

"Padhai dhang se kar raha hai na?" (You're studying properly, right?)

That's her favorite sentence. It doesn't matter if I'm eating, sleeping, or just sitting—she will always find a way to ask this question.

We don't have a lot of money, but we have dreams. And those dreams rest on my shoulders.

The Exhausting Life of a B-Grade College Student

People think college life is fun—bunking classes, hanging out with friends, enjoying freedom.

Not for me.

Because I was in Bal Dayal College—where classes were optional, and attendance was a joke. If I had depended on that college for my education, I would have ended up knowing nothing except how to sign my name on the exam sheet.

So, my actual learning happened outside of college.

Every day, my schedule looked something like this:

- 5:30 AM – Wake up and somehow convince my half-dead body to leave the bed.
- 6:00 AM to 9:00 AM – Maths coaching. Three hours of solving numbers until my brain started seeing algebraic equations in my dreams.
- 9:30 AM to 12:30 PM – Chemistry coaching. Learning about molecules, reactions, and the fact that my life was slowly turning into a periodic table of exhaustion.
- 1:00 PM to 5:00 PM – College. Or as I liked to call it, "attendance duty."

By the time I got home in the evening, my body felt like it had been run over by a truck. But my day wasn't over yet.

How I Earned My Own Pocket Money

Unlike most of my classmates, I couldn't afford to waste money on fancy cafés, branded clothes, or unlimited mobile data. Every rupee mattered.

So, I started teaching students up to Class 8 to cover my daily expenses.

At first, it was just one or two kids from my neighbourhood. But soon, word spread that "Romi Bhaiya is a topper and teaches really well." Parents started sending their kids to me, and before I knew it, I had five students.

I charged a small fee—just enough to buy stationery, books, and the occasional samosa from the roadside stall. But more than the money, teaching gave me something else—respect.

For the first time, I felt independent. I wasn't just a student anymore; I was a teacher. And that meant something.

The Greatest Gift – My First Mobile Phone

Up until then, I had never owned a phone.

Whenever I needed to use one, I had to borrow my father's Nokia, which looked like it had survived multiple world wars. It had a tiny screen, a keypad that required Hulk-like strength to press, and a ringtone that sounded like an ambulance siren.

But then, one evening, my mother surprised me.

She placed a small box in my hand and said, "Ye tere liye." (This is for you.)

I opened it and there it was—a brand new Micromax Q339.

Okay, maybe "brand new" was a bit of an exaggeration. It had 512 MB RAM and 1 GB ROM, which meant it could barely handle two apps without freezing. But for me, it was the greatest gift in the world.

I was officially a mobile phone owner.

I spent the whole night setting it up, installing WhatsApp, and customizing my wallpaper (which was just a motivational quote saying "Success is the only option").

Then I opened my contacts list.

There were 35 numbers in total. Out of those, 30 were family members—chachas, mamis, cousins, and even my grandfather, who never picked up calls but still wanted to be included.

The remaining 5 were my tuition students' parents.

And that was it.

No school friends. No coaching friends. And definitely no female names.

No Female Interactions – The Story of My Life

I had never talked to a girl properly in my entire life.

Not because I didn't want to, but because I never had the chance. My entire existence revolved around books, exams, and coaching classes. Girls were like scientific theories to me—mentioned in textbooks but never seen in real life.

Whenever I saw my classmates casually talking to girls, I felt like they were speaking a language I didn't understand. What do people even talk about? How do you start a conversation?

And more importantly—what if she replies, and I don't know what to say next?

I wasn't shy. I just… lacked experience.

But at that time, I didn't care much. My life was about studies, responsibilities, and proving myself. Relationships, crushes, love—those were things for people who had time to breathe.

And I didn't.

But soon, that was going to change.

Because in the middle of my boring, disciplined, topper life, someone was about to enter.

Munmun.

And my story was about to take a turn I never expected.

Question for the readers
1. What is your opinion about female interaction? Is it necessary? Will it change a boy's personality that no exposure can do?
2. Does College matter? Or Romii is just overthinking about his future?

Chapter 3: First Meet with Munmun

I had spent years mastering the art of avoiding eye contact with girls. Not because I hated them, but because I never knew what to say. My conversations with the opposite gender were limited to basic classroom interactions like "Pass the notebook" or "Sir is calling you."

And yet, that day, as I stood in the college corridor, staring at Munmun, I knew something had changed.

It was the first time in my life I wanted to talk to a girl.

The Moment I Saw Her

The afternoon sun cast a golden glow on her face, making her silky black hair shine as if woven with sunlight. Her deep brown eyes had a softness that made my heart skip a beat. She wasn't the kind of beauty you find in magazines—she was real, effortless, and had an innocence that made her even more charming.

Her smile… God, her smile! It wasn't just a curve on her lips—it was a feeling. A feeling that made me forget the heat, my boring college, and even my stupid CGPA of 9.4, which had pushed me into this mess in the first place.

For a second, I thought I was hallucinating.

Was she really standing there? Here? In Bal Dayal College?

Flashback – School Days

Munmun and I were in the same school, but our worlds had never collided.

She was the kind of girl who had a hundred friends, a lively personality, and an easy laugh. I, on the other hand, was the serious, bookish guy who always sat in the front row, solving math problems while everyone else was busy talking.

If our class was a Bollywood movie, she was the heroine, and I was probably some background character who existed only to fill the classroom.

I had noticed her back then, of course. Who wouldn't? But I never dared to talk to her. Not even once.

And now, after all these years, she was standing in front of me.

And this time, I wasn't going to let the moment slip.

The First Conversation

Just as I was preparing to introduce myself, she spoke first.

"Romi?" she said, tilting her head slightly, as if trying to recognize me.

I nodded, feeling like I had just won a national award because Munmun actually knew my name.

"Oh wow! You're in this college too?" she asked, smiling.

I cleared my throat. "Uh... yeah. Kind of forced into it."

She laughed. "Same here! I wanted to go to St. Xavier's, but my parents chose this college for me."

For a moment, I forgot my hatred for Bal Dayal College. Because if this place had brought Munmun into my life, maybe it wasn't that bad after all.

"What stream?" I asked.

"Commerce," she said casually.

Commerce.

At that moment, I questioned all my life choices.

Why had I taken Science? Why had I agreed to suffer through Chemistry and Physics when I could have just taken Commerce and sat in the same class as Munmun?

She could see the regret on my face because she giggled and said, "Science? Tough choice. Best of luck!"

Great. She probably thought I was one of those nerds who loved solving equations for fun.

Before I could say anything, her friend Neha decided to ruin the moment.

The Neha Problem

Neha was Munmun's best friend from school. She was loud, overconfident, and had a constant smirk on her face that made me dislike her instantly.

I didn't even know her properly, but I already hated how she interrupted our conversation with "Arrey, let's go, Munmun. We're getting late."

She looked at me once, up and down, as if trying to evaluate my worth, then turned away as if I was invisible.

I wanted to tell her, "Bhai, at least pretend I exist."

But I stayed quiet.

Munmun smiled at me once before leaving, saying, "We'll talk later!"

Those three words made my entire day.

A Cycle vs. A Scooty

As I watched Munmun and Neha walks towards the parking area, I saw her take out her scooty keys.

A scooty.

And here I was, standing with my old, second-hand cycle, which made a squeaky sound every time I pedalled.

For the first time, I felt ashamed of my cycle.

While Munmun zoomed off on her stylish two-wheeler, I climbed onto my cycle, trying to avoid eye contact with people so that no one would see the topper of the school riding a near-dead bicycle.

But despite all that, I wasn't upset.

Because for the first time, I wasn't thinking about my mobile.

I was thinking about Munmun.

The Lame Jokes Attempt

The next day, I was determined to make an impression.

I had no idea how to do that, so I did what I had seen other boys do—crack jokes.

The only problem? My jokes were terrible.

When I saw Munmun sitting in the college canteen, I casually walked up to her and said, "You know, I should have taken Commerce instead of Science."

She raised an eyebrow. "Why?"

I smirked. "Because I just realized Commerce students have the best assets."

For a moment, there was complete silence.

Then she burst out laughing.

Not a fake laugh. Not a polite chuckle. A real, genuine, happy laugh.

I had never felt prouder of myself.

For the next few minutes, I kept throwing random, lame jokes, and to my surprise, she laughed at most of them. I didn't care if they were actually funny—I was too busy watching her smile.

For the first time, I understood why boys made fools of themselves in front of girls.

Because when she smiled, it was worth it.

Cloud Nine – The Contact Number Moment

That evening, as I was about to leave for home, Munmun stopped me.

"Hey, Romi, give me your number."

For a second, I thought I had misheard her.

"M-my number?" I stammered.

She nodded. "Yeah, we should stay in touch, right?"

I had never typed digits so fast in my life.

When I finally saved her contact, I looked at my mobile screen, staring at her name.

Munmun.

I had her number.

I had her number!

As I rode my cycle back home, I didn't care about the squeaky noise anymore. I didn't care about Bal Dayal College, my coaching classes, or even my boring Science stream.

Because that day, I wasn't just a topper.

I was a boy who had Munmun's number.

And for now, that was enough.

Question for the readers

1. Have you ever had a crush on someone? I know it's yes. But the question is whether you ever look it as a sin or just enjoyed it a motto of go with the flow?

2. Do you believe one conversation can change the way you see a person forever?

Chapter 4: The Talking Stage

I had Munmun's number in my phone.

It was there, saved in my contact list, between "Mummy" and "Mama Ji," as if it was just another name. But it wasn't. It was the most important name in my entire phone.

For the first time in my life, I had the opportunity to text a girl.

But there was just one problem.

I didn't know if I should.

The Great Dilemma: To Text or Not to Text

I sat on my bed, staring at my phone screen like it was a bomb that would explode the moment I pressed "send." My thumb hovered over the keyboard, my brain screaming with self-doubt.

What if she thinks I'm desperate?

What if she ignores my message?

What if she laughs at me with her friends?

I had spent my whole life being a studious, serious boy, and suddenly, I was behaving like one of those "Lover boys" who forgot their syllabus the moment they saw a pretty girl.

I could already imagine my Sigma male version scolding me:

"Arrey, topper ho! Koi majboori hai kya? Why should you text first?"

For the next two hours, I kept opening and closing WhatsApp, convincing myself that she should text first. After all, wasn't she the one who asked for my number?

But then another thought struck me.

What if she was also waiting for me to text?

What if she thought I wasn't interested?

That's when I realized… this was a war, and my ego was the enemy.

The First Text

After what felt like a century of overthinking, I finally gathered the courage to type a message.

"Hii."

Just that. No extra words, no emojis—simple, safe, and easy to ignore if she wanted to.

The moment I hit send, I slammed my phone face down on the bed as if I had committed a crime. My heart started racing.

I tried to focus on my books, but suddenly, Newton's laws of motion felt useless. All I cared about was one thing:

Would Munmun reply?

The Waiting Game

Every few minutes, I peeked at my phone screen, hoping to see a notification. But nothing.

I started panicking.

What if I had messed up? Maybe I should have added an emoji? Maybe I should have said, "Hey, remember me? Romi from school!" instead of just "Hii"?

I had never waited for a message this desperately in my life. Even during exam results, I was calmer.

And then, it happened.

The screen lit up.

Munmun: "Hii Romi! How are you?"

I forgot how to breathe.

She replied.

She actually replied!

I was so happy, I wanted to frame the message and put it on my wall like a trophy.

The First Conversation

What started as a simple text turned into a full-hour conversation.

For the first time, I wasn't talking about marks, syllabus, or career plans. I was talking to a girl about random things—college life, school memories, even the weather!

And it felt... nice.

Munmun was funny, easy to talk to, and had a way of making every conversation light-hearted.

At one point, she sent a laughing emoji in response to one of my jokes, and I swear, my soul left my body for a moment.

It was the first time in my life I smiled like an idiot because of a text.

The Change in Me

That night, as I lay in bed, I realized something.

I was changing.

I had always been the topper, the boy who only cared about grades, coaching classes, and exams. But now? Now I was checking my phone every five minutes, waiting for Munmun's reply.

For the first time in my life, studies weren't my top priority.

Was this what it felt like to fall for someone?

I didn't know.

All I knew was that I was happy.

And that scared me a little.

Boys These Days…

I had always laughed at boys who changed the moment they got attention from a girl. They started dressing better, listening to romantic songs, and posting deep quotes on WhatsApp status.

"Pyaar me pad gaye hai ye log," I used to joke.

But now?

Now I was checking my phone twenty times a day, waiting for a girl's messages.

Now I understood why those boys acted that way.

Because when a girl like Munmun enters your life, you don't remain the same.

But what about her?

As much as I was enjoying this new phase, there was one thing I didn't know.

What was she thinking?

Was she also smiling while texting me?

Did she also wait for my messages the way I waited for hers?

Or was I just another friend to her?

I didn't have the answer.

All I had was my side of the story.

And for now, that was enough.

Question for the readers
1. Do you ever overthink before sending a text to someone you like?
2. How do you know when you're just talking to someone and when you're actually falling for them?

Chapter 5: Shaima

There are some things in life you just can't talk about with everyone.

Crushes, feelings, love—all these topics need a special person to discuss. Someone who won't judge, someone who will listen, and someone who will either support you or roast you mercilessly—depending on their mood.

For me, that person was Shaima.

Meet Shaima: The Relationship Expert

Shaima was my cousin—the same age as me but miles ahead in terms of life experience. If love and relationships were a college course, she had already completed her PhD while I was still figuring out the syllabus.

She had seen it all—the excitement of a new relationship, the drama, the fights, the breakups, and the late-night crying sessions over sad songs.

If anyone could guide me through this unknown world of feelings, it was her.

So, one evening, as we sat on the terrace, I decided to tell her about Munmun.

"Ooo, Bhai Ko Pyaar Ho Gaya!"

The moment I took Munmun's name, Shaima's eyes lit up like she had just heard the juiciest gossip of the year.

"Areee! So, finally, my dear cousin has a girlfriend!" she teased, poking my arm.

"Shut up! She's not my girlfriend!" I protested, feeling my ears turn red.

"Oh please," she smirked. "First, you stare at her. Then you get her number. Then you start waiting for her messages. Next thing you know, you'll be writing poetry about her."

I sighed. This was a bad idea.

The Wise Advice

After a good five minutes of teasing me, Shaima finally calmed down.

"Okay, okay, tell me," She said, leaning forward. "What exactly is happening?"

I told her everything—how I met Munmun again, how we started texting, how my studies were getting affected, and how I smiled like an idiot every time she replied.

Shaima listened carefully, nodding like a love guru.

"Look, bhai," she finally said. "I'm happy for you. But just remember one thing—don't lose yourself in this. Pyar achha lagta hai, par agar padhai barbaad ho gayi, toh mummy-papa teri jaan le lenge."

She wasn't wrong. My marks were my biggest identity, and if I messed them up because of my new WhatsApp addiction, I would never forgive myself.

"Balance is important," she added. "Enjoy the feeling, but don't let it control you."

It made sense. But there was something else bothering me.

Some Things Are Just... Personal

Even though Shaima was my closest person, I still felt uncomfortable sharing too much about my so called crush.

I could tell her the basic details, but there were some things that felt too special to talk about.

Like the way Munmun's hair fell over her face when she laughed.

Like the silly jokes we shared that only we understood.

Like the way my heart raced whenever I saw her name pop up on my screen.

These things were mine.

And for the first time in my life, I understood why people say, "Some feelings can't be explained, only felt."

The Importance of a Confidant

That night, as I lay in bed, I realized how lucky I was to have Shaima.

Not everyone has someone to talk to about these emotions.

Love, crushes, heartbreaks—these are all new and confusing experiences, and without the right guidance, people either mess up their studies or mess up their relationships.

Shaima made sure I did neither.

I didn't know what was going to happen between me and Munmun, but at least I knew one thing—

No matter how things turned out, I had someone to talk to.

And sometimes, that makes all the difference.

Question for the readers
1. Do you have someone in your life who understands you better than you understand yourself?
2. How much should you share about your inner feelings with others, and how much should you keep to yourself?

Chapter 6: A Word from Shaima

There's something you should know about Romi.

The way he tells his story—filled with emotions, self-doubt, overthinking, and occasional foolishness—makes it seem like he's just another typical teenage boy who has fallen for a girl and is struggling to figure out his emotions.

But let me tell you the truth.

Romi is not a typical teenage boy.

He is different.

And I, Shaima, his cousin, best friend, and unofficial life coach, am here to tell you why.

The Romi I Have Known Since Childhood

Romi has always been special.

While other kids in our neighborhood ran around playing cricket in the streets, Romi sat with his school books, solving math problems that weren't even in our syllabus.

While we all struggled to pass with average marks, he was the kid who would panic if he scored anything less than 90%.

His dedication, sincerity, and discipline set him apart. And let's be honest, it also made him a little boring.

"Bhai, take a break," I would say. "Come play with us!"

"No, I have to complete this chapter," he would reply, without even looking up from his book.

At that time, we all thought Romi was obsessed with studies.

But later, I realized—he wasn't just studying for himself.

He was studying for his family.

A Boy with Responsibilities

Unlike many of us, Romi didn't have the luxury of ignoring reality.

His father worked as a waiter at Hotel Samridhi International, a job that required him to stand for hours, serving customers with a polite smile.

His mother was a housewife, managing everything within the limited income they had.

Romi had no choice but to succeed.

He knew that his studies were his only ticket out of struggle.

That's why, while we all wasted time watching TV or scrolling on our cheap Android phones, Romi spent his evenings teaching kids to earn some extra money for his daily expenses.

He was just 16 years old, but he already carried the burden of an adult.

The Day Romi Told Me About Munmun

The day Romi told me about Munmun, I was honestly shocked.

Not because he liked a girl—he's human, after all. But because he told me.

Romi was never the type to talk about feelings. He could solve complex equations in seconds but struggled to understand the mathematics of emotions.

So, when he nervously mentioned Munmun's name, I immediately knew—

This was serious.

"So, bhai finally has a girlfriend?" I teased, watching his ears turn red.

"She's not my girlfriend," he mumbled, looking away.

That's when I saw it.

That smile.

The stupid, dreamy, lovestruck smile that every guy gets when he likes a girl.

And in that moment, I understood—

For the first time in his life, Romi was distracted.

My Own Love Story—And What I Learned

I never opposed Romi's feelings for Munmun.

Why would I? I had been through the same phase myself.

Back in school, I was in a relationship too. It was sweet, full of innocent texting, secret glances in class, and dreams of a future together.

But then, reality hit.

Major issues started piling up—family pressure, career choices, and different priorities.

We realized that love alone was not enough.

So, we broke up.

It wasn't dramatic. There were no fights, no betrayal— just a mutual understanding that we had to focus on our futures.

It hurt. A lot. But it also taught me a lesson.

And that's the lesson I wanted Romi to understand before it was too late.

A Reminder, Not a Warning

I never told Romi to stay away from Munmun.

I simply reminded him of his priorities.

"Feelings are great, bhai," I told him. "But don't forget why you started this journey."

Munmun might be his present happiness, but his family, education, and future were the things that defined him.

"You have a responsibility, Romi," I said. "You're the one who will change your family's life. Don't let one distraction ruin everything you've worked for."

He didn't say much.

He just nodded.

And that's when I knew—he understood.

The Truth About Love and Life

Love is a beautiful thing.

But love without stability, goals, and maturity is just an illusion.

I don't know where Romi's story with Munmun will go.

But I know this—

No matter what happens, he will always be Romi—the boy who refuses to be left behind.

And that's what makes him special.

Question for the readers

1. Do you think people change when they fall in love? Or do they just become more of who they really are?

2. If you had the chance to warn your younger self about love, what would you do?

Chapter 7: The Smiling Ride

Some days start just like any other—nothing special, nothing extraordinary.

But by the time they end, you realize that something inside you has changed.

Something so unexpected and beautiful happens that you can't stop thinking about it.

For me, this was that day.

Munmun's Scooty—A Royal Ride

Before I tell you what happened, let me introduce you to a very important character in this chapter.

No, not Munmun. You already know about her.

I'm talking about her Honda Activa scooty.

Yes, it wasn't just a two-wheeler—it was a statement.

A black, glossy, always-clean scooty that she rode like a queen gliding through her kingdom.

She never rode too fast nor too slow. It was as if the scooty obeyed her command perfectly.

And whenever she entered the college parking area, something strange happened—time slowed down.

Boys turned their heads, girls admired her confidence, and I... I just stood there like a fool, pretending not to look.

But today, fate had different plans.

Because today, for the first time, I wouldn't just be watching Munmun ride her scooty.

I would be sitting behind her.

Yes. Me. Romi. The shy topper.

Destiny works in mysterious ways, doesn't it?

A Cycle Disaster and a Lucky Coincidence

The day didn't start on a positive note.

I was all set to leave for college when my cycle betrayed me.

As soon as I sat on it and pedaled, the chain got stuck.

It refused to move.

I bent down, tried to fix it, applied some oil, even kicked it in frustration.

But nothing worked.

"Arey, kya ho gaya?" my mother asked, peeking from the window.

"Cycle ki chain kharab ho gayi," I muttered, wiping my greasy hands on a cloth.

"Toh auto le lo, late ho jaoge," she suggested.

I sighed. There was no other option.

So, I locked my betrayer cycle in the garage and took an auto-rickshaw to college.

Little did I know that this small inconvenience was actually become a blessing in disguise.

Avikal and Amit—My Brothers from Another Mother

As soon as I reached college, I met Avikal and Amit.

They weren't just my friends. They were my lifelines.

We had been together since school days, and even though we had taken different streams now, our bond remained unbreakable.

Avikal was the funny one. He always had something sarcastic to say.

Amit, on the other hand, was the calm one. He spoke less, but whenever he did, it made sense.

And yet, despite being so close to them, I had never told them about Munmun.

I only gave small hints.

"Bhai, college me koi special dost bana ya nahi?" Avikal had asked me once.

"Haan, ek hai," I had replied casually, avoiding eye contact.

But I never revealed the name.

Because some things are too precious to share.

Munmun's Unexpected Offer

After college, as I was about to walk towards the auto stand, I heard a familiar voice.

"Romi!"

I turned around, and there she was.

Munmun.

Standing beside her scooty, looking at me with curiosity.

"Where's your cycle?" she asked, tilting her head slightly.

For a second, I forgot how to breathe.

The evening sun was setting behind her, and its golden light made her eyes shine even brighter.

Her silky hair moved slightly in the breeze, and her lips curled into a small, playful smile.

God, was she even real?

"Wo... aaj uski chain puri tarah se kharab ho gayi thi," I finally managed to say, cursing myself for not having a cooler response.

"Ohh... toh ab kaise jaaoge?" she asked.

"Auto se," I replied.

She thought for a moment and then said something that sent my heart racing.

"Chalo, main drop kar deti hoon."

I blinked. Once. Twice.

Did she just say she'll drop me?

Did I hear that correctly?

I almost wanted to look up at the sky and check if God was in a generous mood today.

"Neha aaj nahi aayi, toh main akeli hoon. Tumhe drop karna koi badi baat nahi hai," she added casually.

Oh, Neha!

For the first time in my life, I thanked Neha for her absence.

I glanced at Avikal and Amit.

They were both staring at me as if I had just won a lottery.

"Bhai, kya scene hai?" Avikal whispered.

I shrugged, trying to hide my inner excitement.

"Chalo na," Munmun said, adjusting her scooty's mirror.

And just like that, my dream ride began.

The Ride from Bal Dayal College to Buddha Colony

Sitting behind Munmun on her scooty was both the best and scariest experience of my life.

I had never sat this close to a girl before.

I kept my hands firmly on my lap, afraid to even move.

"Romi, relax. Main racing bike thodi chala rahi hoon," she laughed.

I nodded, though my heart was beating faster than her scooty's engine.

As we rode through the streets, her hair occasionally brushed against my face.

It smelled of fruity shampoo—a mix of mango and something sweet.

With every turn, I could feel her soft presence in front of me.

For the first time in my life, I understood why people called it a dream ride.

From Bal Dayal College to Buddha Colony, I forgot about everything—my studies, my CGPA, my B-grade college.

All that mattered was this moment.

A simple ride home with the girl who had unknowingly become the most special part of my life.

Question for the readers
1. Have you ever been so close to someone that you could feel your heart racing, yet they had no idea?
2. Does the way someone looks at you change the way you see yourself?

Chapter 8: Old is Gold

Some friendships are like newly bought clothes—fresh, exciting, and full of charm.

And then, there are friendships that are like your oldest, most comfortable t-shirt—slightly faded but irreplaceable.

For me, that old t-shirt was Avikal and Amit.

Yes, I had met Munmun. Yes, my life had taken an unexpected turn.

But there were two constants in my life.

And their names were Avikal and Amit.

Avikal—More Than a Friend, Like a Brother

If you ever needed a perfect example of the phrase "paise ka ghamand nahi tha, par paise ka confidence tha", it was Avikal.

He belonged to a high-middle-class family. They had a big house, cars, and enough relatives to make a full cricket team.

Unlike my small nuclear family, Avikal lived in a joint family, where his Chachu (uncle) was like the CEO of the house.

"Bhai, hamare yahan koi bhi chiz lene se pehle Chachu se permission leni padti hai," he once said.

"Matlab agar Maggi khani ho toh bhi?" Amit asked.

"Haan, pehle unko batana padta hai. Phir woh Papa se discuss karte hain. Phir Dadi apna verdict deti hain. Tab jaake kitchen se Maggi nikalne ki permission milti hai," Avikal said with a sigh.

"Bhai, yeh toh sarkari daftar jaisa hai," I laughed.

But despite coming from a privileged background, Avikal was never arrogant.

He was the kind of friend who would spend thousands on a new phone but still happily eat roadside chaat with us.

And most importantly, he was the kind of friend who had stood by me through every phase of life.

When my father lost his job for three months, and I was struggling to manage my tuition fees, it was Avikal who secretly slipped ₹500 in my bag.

"Arey bhai, lottery lagi thi. Extra paisa pada tha, soch raha tha kis par ehsaan karu," he had said casually, pretending it was no big deal.

That's how he was.

Always helping without making it feel like help.

That's why, even though we were just friends, I always felt like he was my big brother.

Amit—The Underestimated Genius

If Avikal was a businessman's son, then Amit was the son of an honest government clerk.

He came from a middle-class family, where saving money was an art, and spending money was a crime.

He wasn't as privileged as Avikal, nor was he as studious as me.

But his brain?

Sharper than a brand-new Gillette razor blade.

The problem was, his intelligence never reflected in his report card.

He was one of those students who never studied but always found a way to pass.

"Bhai, main syllabus nahi padhta. Main teacher ka dimaag padhta hoon," he once explained.

"Matlab?" I asked.

"Matlab main dekh leta hoon ki teacher kis topic par zyada focus kar raha hai. Usi pe tik mark lagata hoon aur wahi exam me likh ke aa jata hoon," he smirked.

And surprisingly, this technique worked!

Amit had a street-smart brain. He could fix anything—bikes, mobiles, even relationships.

"Bhai, agar koi ladki gussa ho toh bas ek hi cheez kaam karega," he once said.

"Kya?" Avikal and I leaned in, expecting some philosophical wisdom.

"Uske baal ki tareef karo," Amit declared like a love guru.

"Kya logic hai bhai?" I laughed.

"Logic simple hai. Baal ka tareef koi bhi ladki ignore nahi kar sakti," Amit said confidently.

I didn't know whether to believe him or not, but later when I met Munmun, I actually tried it once.

And guess what? It worked.

That day, I realized that Amit wasn't just a friend.

He was a genius ahead of his time.

The Great Google Maps Disaster

One of my favourite memories with Avikal and Amit was the day we got completely lost in the city.

It was monsoon season, and our college had just started.

Since none of us were familiar with the college route, we decided to use Google Maps.

Bad idea.

Very bad idea.

We were on our cycles, navigating through the busy Patna roads, when Google Maps decided to act like a toxic ex—giving us false hope and then betraying us.

"Turn left in 500 meters," the robotic voice said.

We followed it obediently.

"Turn right in 200 meters," it instructed again.

We obeyed like loyal soldiers.

After 15 minutes, we realized we had been going in circles.

Amit, who was holding my phone for directions, scratched his head.

"Bhai... ek minute... ye toh wahi gali hai na jisme hum pehle bhi aaye the?" Avikal asked.

We all looked around.

Yes.

We had officially entered a loop.

"Saala Google ne ghumake rakha hai," Amit muttered.

But the real tragedy happened when it suddenly started raining heavily.

And guess where we got stuck?

In an area where the roads were completely covered with muddy water.

We tried to move forward, but the water was so deep that our cycles got stuck.

"Bhai, agar yahi haal raha, toh aaj ghar jaane ke liye Titanic ki zaroorat padegi," Avikal joked, trying to push his cycle out.

Amit, on the other hand, had given up.

"Main bas yahi baith jaata hoon. Jab barish rukegi tab dekh lenge," he said, parking himself on a dry spot.

I checked my phone. The internet was gone.

Google Maps had abandoned us in our worst time.

Finally, after struggling for half an hour, we asked a local uncle for help, who pointed us to a shortcut back to the main road.

That day, we learned a valuable lesson.

Never trust Google Maps blindly.

And if you ever get lost, just ask an uncle.

They know everything.

New Friend, Old Bonds

Yes, I had a special friend now.

Yes, my focus had shifted.

But no matter how many new people entered my life, Avikal and Amit would always be irreplaceable.

Because at the end of the day, new friendships bring excitement.

But old friendships bring comfort.

And in this world full of temporary people, old friends are the real gold.

Question for the readers

1. Have you ever realized the value of old friendships only after life took you in different directions?

2. Why do we sometimes chase new things, only to realize that what we truly needed was always with us?

Chapter 9: The Confession

There are moments in life when time slows down.

Not because of some scientific phenomenon, but because your heart is stuck between hope and fear.

And for me, this was one of those moments.

I was about to do something that could either make my life beautiful or make everything awkward forever.

I was about to confess my feelings to Munmun.

Typing… Deleting… Typing Again…
It had been months since I started talking to Munmun.

Our conversations had turned from casual texts to long, late-night chats filled with laughter.

I knew one thing for sure—I liked her.

But saying it was an entirely different battle.

Not because I had any doubt.

But because the world we lived in made it difficult for boys to confess their feelings.

Society teaches us that boys are supposed to be fearless, strong, and confident.

But when it comes to expressing emotions, suddenly, the same society starts judging us.

"Ladka hi pehle bolega toh ajeeb lagega," some people say.

"Agar ladki ne na bol diya toh respect chali jayegi," others warn.

It wasn't about courage. It was about consequences.

What if she stopped talking to me?

What if she felt uncomfortable?

What if she laughed at me?

Amit once said, "Bhai, hum ladko ke liye pyaar express karna ek tarah ka suicide mission hota hai."

That night, I opened WhatsApp.

I clicked on Munmun's chat.

I typed: "Munmun, I love you."

And then I deleted it.

"Too much," I thought.

I tried again: "Munmun, I have feelings for you."

Deleted again.

"Sounds too dramatic."

Finally, after an hour of overthinking, I typed:

"Munmun, I started liking you."

Simple. No pressure.

And before my coward brain could stop me, I pressed send.

And then... the longest wait of my life began.

The 16 Hours of Torture

After pressing send, I stared at my phone like a man staring at a ticking bomb.

Two blue ticks appeared.

She saw it.

But… no reply.

Maybe she's busy.

Maybe she's sleeping.

Maybe she's thinking about how to reply.

Each minute felt like an hour.

Each hour felt like a day.

After two hours, I started considering worst-case scenarios.

What if she blocks me?

What if she shows my text to Neha?

What if tomorrow, the whole college starts calling me "cheap" for confessing first?

I switched off my phone.

I decided to not check WhatsApp for the whole night.

But who was I fooling?

I turned it back on within 10 minutes.

Still no reply.

At 2 AM, I lay in my bed, staring at the ceiling, feeling more nervous than I had ever felt in an exam hall.

"Bhai, science ka student hoon, aur ye chhoti si equation solve nahi ho rahi," I muttered to myself.

Finally, at 5 AM, exhaustion took over, and I fell asleep.

Avoiding Eye Contact at College

The next morning, I woke up with a sick feeling in my stomach.

Still no reply from Munmun.

I got ready, but for the first time, I wasn't excited about going to college.

Instead, I was terrified.

What if she ignored me?

What if she told Neha everything?

As I entered the college gate, my eyes automatically started searching for Munmun.

I spotted her scooty parked near the entrance.

"Toh aayi toh hai college," I thought.

But I didn't have the courage to face her.

I avoided the usual places where we met.

I took longer routes to reach class, just to avoid passing near her.

Even when I saw her from a distance, I pretended to look at my phone or talk to random classmates.

My heart was racing.

Did she read my text and decide to never talk to me again?

Or was she just waiting for the right moment to reply?

I was too scared to find out.

Why Is It So Hard for Boys?

That day, as I sat in class, staring at the blackboard but not really seeing anything, I had a thought.

Why is it so hard for a boy to express his emotions?

Why do we feel like we are committing a crime just by saying "I like you" to someone?

If a girl confesses, it's seen as cute, bold, and romantic.

But when a boy does the same, it's seen as cheap, desperate, and weak.

People say, "Arey, ladka pehle propose karega toh uski izzat kam ho jayegi."

But why?

Why is love seen as a one-sided battlefield where the boy has to fight with his own fears, society's judgment, and the risk of losing a friend?

The truth is, most boys are not afraid of rejection.

They are afraid of being misunderstood.

They are afraid that one wrong word can ruin everything.

And that fear… is what makes confessions the hardest thing in the world.

Back to Reality

After spending the whole day in mental torture, I finally checked my phone again in the evening.

Still no reply.

It had been 16 hours.

16 hours of doubt, regret, overthinking, and anxiety.

And then, just when I was about to lose all hope...

My phone vibrated.

1 new message from Munmun.

My heart stopped.

I took a deep breath.

And with shaking hands, I opened the message.

Question for the readers

1. Is Confessing your feelings at your teenage a bad thing?

2. What is your opinion about Romi's mindset? Will that confession make him a bad boy?

Chapter 10:
The Confusion and the Future Goals

Some moments in life feel like standing on the edge of a cliff. You don't know whether you'll fall or fly.

Opening Munmun's message was exactly that moment for me.

For 16 straight hours, I had lived through an emotional rollercoaster—hope, fear, overthinking, regret, anxiety, excitement—all combined into one massive heart attack.

And now, here I was, sitting on my bed, staring at my phone, too scared to open WhatsApp.

"Bhai, bas khol le na!" my inner voice screamed.

"Nahi bhai, kya pata kya likha ho," another voice in my head argued.

This wasn't just a text message.

This was my fate, my future, my entire izzat in one notification.

If it was a rejection, I would be dead inside.

If it was a positive reply, I would be reborn as Shah Rukh Khan from Om Shanti Om.

And if it was something confusing, well... then I would continue being a miserable, overthinking 16-year-old.

After ten minutes of building up courage, I finally opened it.

Munmun's Reply – A Masterpiece of Confusion

Her message read:

"Romi, I saw you in college today, but I guess you were not interested in talking to me?"

And then she added:

"Anyway, you're my best friend, and I'll always be with you forever :)"

I read the message.

Then I read it again.

Then I stared at my phone like it was a complicated math problem with no solution.

WHAT. THE. HELL. DID. THIS. MEAN?

Friendzone or Something More?

Best friend?? Forever??

Did I just get friendzoned?

Or was this one of those secret messages that girls send, which require Sherlock Holmes-level decoding?

Was it a yes?

Was it a no?

Was it a "Let's see what happens in the future"?

"Bhai, iske aage to Quadratic Equation ki complexity bhi kam hai," I muttered to myself.

This is why I always say—girls have a PhD in confusing boys.

If a boy likes a girl, he simply says:

"I like you."

"I love you."

"Will you be my girlfriend?"

But when a girl responds, she unlocks a whole new level of mystery.

For example:

Boy: "Do you like me?"

Girl: "I like talking to you."

Haan toh matlab haan hai ya nahi?

Another classic:

Boy: "I love you."

Girl: "You are such a sweet person."

Bhai, main sweet lag raha hoon ya sugar-free lag raha hoon, yeh toh batao!

And now, Munmun's reply had done exactly this to me.

Overthinking Mode: ON

After reading her message, my mind went into hyper-overthinking mode.

1. Maybe she called me her best friend just to make me feel comfortable?

2. Maybe "forever" means she actually likes me, but she's waiting for me to say something more?

3. Or maybe… just maybe… I have just entered the Friendzone Headquarters, and my application has been approved?

I needed a girl translator.

Unfortunately, Google Translate doesn't offer a "Decode Girl's Messages" option.

I felt like a scientist trying to crack the meaning of life.

But before my brain could explode, something unexpected happened.

From Overthinking to Bollywood Dreams

After a few minutes of intense analysis, my brain did what every boy's brain does in such situations—it started dreaming.

Suddenly, I wasn't just Romi from Patna anymore.

I was Uday Chopra from Dhoom dreaming about Bipasha Basu.

Wearing a cool leather jacket, riding Munmun's scooty like it was a superbike, and saying cringy yet romantic dialogues like:

"Aankhon mein dekh apni tasveer, dil ke darpan mein dekh apni taqdeer!"

Meanwhile, Munmun, dressed in a red saree like Aishwarya Rai, would say:

"Romi, tumse achha kaun hai?"

And together, we would ride into the sunset, while "Dilbara" played in the background.

Yes, I had officially lost it.

Reality Strikes Again

Just as I was about to plan our honeymoon in Switzerland, my phone buzzed.

A message from Amit:

"Bhai, kal coaching pe time pe aana. Sir phir se late aaye toh tu hi padha dena."

And just like that, my Bollywood dream shattered into pieces.

I was still Romi from Patna, not Uday Chopra.

Munmun was still Munmun, and I still had no idea whether she liked me or not.

But one thing was clear—we were still talking.

And that meant the story wasn't over yet.

Maybe she liked me.

Maybe she didn't.

Maybe she was just waiting for the right moment.

All I could do was wait and see.

Final Thoughts

The confusion was still there.

But you know what? That was okay.

Because sometimes, life isn't about getting answers immediately.

Sometimes, it's about enjoying the journey, the uncertainty, the little moments.

And in that moment, as I lay on my bed, still smiling like an idiot, I realized—

Even if I didn't have all the answers,

At least, I was having one hell of a story to tell.

Question for the readers
1. Have you ever daydreamed like Romi? If yes, think again about the same daydream. Do you smile or regret after thinking that again?
2. What is your opinion about the role of movies that have created a different fantasy in our mind about love?

Chapter 11: The Caste Issue

Some barriers are visible—like distance, time, or misunderstandings.

But some barriers are invisible yet stronger than walls made of steel.

One such invisible wall was standing right in front of me.

The caste issue

A Love Divided by Caste

I was a Kayasth.

Munmun was a Rajput.

In an ideal world, this shouldn't matter.

But this wasn't an ideal world.

This was 2016, Bihar.

A place where caste was not just a word, but an identity.

A place where people would kill their own happiness just to protect their "honor."

And worst of all—Munmun's father was the guardian of that so-called honor.

The Man with the Swords

I still remember the first time Munmun casually mentioned her father's swords.

"Papa ke paas ek nahi, do-do talwar hai ghar pe."

I had laughed back then. A harmless joke.

But now, when I thought about it, that same joke felt like a death threat.

I imagined myself standing in front of her father, just like Shahrukh Khan in DDLJ, trying to convince Amrish Puri—

But instead of saying, "Ja Simran ja, jee le apni zindagi,"

I was sure Munmun's father would say, "Beta, yeh talwar dekh rahe ho? Yeh tumhare sir ke upar latak rahi hai. Apna dhar (the head) smbhaal kr rkhna"

The thought itself was enough to send chills down my spine.

Munmun's Hesitation

Though Munmun never said anything openly, her actions spoke volumes.

Whenever we talked about relationships, she would either change the topic or laugh it off.

Whenever I jokingly asked, "Agar kisi ne tumse pyaar kiya toh?",

She would just say, "Papa nahi manenge."

Not "Mujhe nahi pasand."

Not "Mujhe pyaar mein interest nahi hai."

Just "Papa nahi manenge."

That meant one thing—somewhere deep inside, she liked me too (thinking just for the sake of my happiness).

But she was scared.

Scared of her family, society, and the expectations that came with her caste.

The Harsh Reality of Caste in Love

This wasn't the first time I had seen love lose against caste.

I had heard real-life stories of people who loved each other but couldn't be together because of their surnames.

Love marriages were already rare in our society.

And even when they happened, they were mostly within the same caste.

People could accept:

- A poor and rich couple.
- A young and old couple.
- Even a jobless and successful couple.

But a Kayasth and a Rajput?

Unacceptable.

The same society that talked about love and unity, was the same society that created walls higher than mountains.

And the worst part?

Nobody even questioned it.

Overthinking Mode: Activated

For the next few days, the thought didn't leave my mind.

I couldn't focus on my studies.

I couldn't enjoy my time with Avikal and Amit.

Because no matter how hard I tried, my heart kept pulling me back to Munmun.

And the more I thought, the more painful it became.

What if she liked me, but would never accept it?

What if, even after all my efforts, this love story would never reach its happy ending?

Would I be able to see her get married to someone else just because that boy had the "right" surname?

Would I be able to move on and forget everything?

Or was this just the beginning of a long, painful journey?

The Unsaid Words

I wanted to ask Munmun.

I wanted to say, "Forget society. Just tell me—do you like me or not?"

But I never did.

Because deep down, I was afraid of her answer.

Afraid that she would say, "Yes, but it doesn't matter."

Afraid that she would say, "Yes, but we can never be together."

Afraid that she would choose society over love.

And most of all, I was afraid because…

I already knew the answer.

I just didn't want to hear it from her mouth.

The Helplessness of a Boy in Love (Or so called 'Love')

People think boys have it easy.

They say, "Ladkon ke paas toh power hota hai, decision hota hai."

But let me tell you—there is nothing more painful than being a boy in love.

Because we are the ones who have to confess.

We are the ones who have to fight.

We are the ones who have to take risks.

And even after all that, we still end up losing.

One rejection from a girl? Game over.

One strict father? Game over.

One caste issue? Game over.

Society had already decided my fate before I even got the chance to fight for it.

I was powerless.

And nothing hurts more than knowing that you love someone but can do absolutely nothing about it.

Final Thoughts

For the first time in my life, I questioned everything.

What was the point of loving someone if society wouldn't let us be together?

What was the point of dreaming of a future with someone if that future was already destroyed before it even began?

Was I being foolish to even think that Munmun and I could be something more than just friends?

Or was I being brave to at least try?

I didn't know the answers.

But one thing was clear—

This wasn't going to be easy.

And if Munmun truly liked me, she would have to fight, too.

Because love is not just about feelings.

It's about standing against the world, even when the world is against you.

Chapter 12: The Mental Blockage

Exams were near.

For most students, this was the most crucial time of their school life—

A time to prove themselves,

A time to focus,

A time to prepare for their future.

But for me, it was something else.

For me, it was a war inside my own mind.

A war between logic and emotion.

Between studies and heartbreak.

The Sudden Disappearance

For the past ten days, there had been complete silence.

No "Good morning" texts.

No "Had lunch?" messages.

No random conversations about college.

And worst of all—no DP on her WhatsApp.

Now, any boy would understand this unsaid rule of social media:

- If a girl removes her DP, something is wrong.

- If a girl posts a sad song on her status, something is seriously wrong.
- And if a girl disappears completely, it's the end of the world.

I checked my phone countless times in those ten days.

But there was nothing.

The Unanswered Questions

"Kya hua hoga?"

"Did I do something wrong?"

"Is she ignoring me?"

"Is she okay?"

Overthinking is a disease, and I was suffering from it badly.

I wanted to text her.

I wanted to ask, "Munmun, sab thik hai?"

But then, another thought hit me—

"What if she doesn't want to talk?"

"What if she is dealing with something personal?"

"What if she finds me irritating?"

My hands would hover over the keyboard… and then I would put my phone away.

Because sometimes, silence is better than getting an answer you don't want to hear.

The Struggle of Science v/s Commerce

The exams started, but another problem arrived—

Science and Commerce shifts were different.

Commerce students had their exams in the morning.

Science students (like me) had their exams in the afternoon.

That meant, zero chance of meeting Munmun during the exams.

Fate was playing games with me.

I would reach college every day and see the Commerce students leaving the exam hall.

And in that crowd of students, somewhere, Munmun was also there.

I saw her a few times from a distance.

But she didn't see me.

Or maybe… she ignored me.

And every time I saw her but didn't talk, the mental blockage inside me grew stronger.

February 26, 2018 – The Last Exam

That day, the Commerce students had their last exam.

For them, the battle was over.

For us (Science students), it was still going on.

I was standing near the main college gate, holding my guess papers in my hand.

Students were running out, excited about their freedom.

I was looking for one face in that crowd.

And then—I saw her.

The Letter

Munmun was walking towards the exit with her friends.

Her scooty keys were in her hand.

I was standing a few meters away, pretending to read my guess paper—

(But in reality, my mind was not even in this world.)

Just when she was about to leave, she turned towards me.

For the first time in ten days, our eyes met.

And before I could react, she walked up to me.

She didn't say anything.

She just took out a folded paper from her notebook and handed it to me.

"Yeh rakhna."

That's all she said.

And before I could ask anything, she left.

I stood there, frozen.

Because this was the first time a girl had ever written something for me.

The Battle of Emotions

My hands were shaking as I held the letter.

What was in it?

Was it a love letter?

Was it a farewell note?

Was it something she wrote out of anger, or out of affection?

Hundreds of thoughts attacked my brain all at once.

I could hear Avikal and Amit calling me from behind, but their voices felt distant.

I had never been this nervous in my life.

Even board exams didn't scare me this much.

I slowly slipped the letter into my pocket and looked around, making sure no one saw it.

Because if someone caught me with a girl's letter, my reputation as a shy, studious boy would be over.

The Walk Back Home

I didn't open the letter immediately.

I don't know why, but I was afraid.

Maybe because I knew—whatever was written inside would change everything.

So, I did the only thing I could do at that moment—

I focussed on my exam and after my paper, I put my headphones in, played a random song, and started walking back home.

But no matter how loud the music was, one thought kept echoing in my mind—

"Is this the beginning of something beautiful... or the end of everything?"

Chapter 13: The Situationship

A Letter That Couldn't Be Opened Freely

I stood in front of my house, staring at the letter Munmun had given me.

It was just a small folded piece of paper, but it felt heavier than my entire Chemistry textbook.

I took a deep breath and walked inside, casually stuffing it into my pocket as if it was nothing.

Because in an Indian family, a teenage boy cannot just openly hold a letter.

If my mother saw it, she would immediately ask, "Yeh kya hai?"

If my father noticed, he would give me a sharp look as if I had committed a crime.

And if my nosy neighbour aunty caught even a glimpse of it, by evening, the entire colony would know that Romi has started getting love letters.

So, like a criminal hiding evidence, I quickly slipped into my room and locked the door.

Finally, I pulled the letter out and unfolded it.

My hands trembled slightly.

For a moment, I just stared at the paper, feeling a strange mix of excitement, fear, and nervousness, just like a mixed vegetable.

Then, I started reading.

The Letter from Munmun

"Romi,"

"I know we are not talking to each other these days… but please don't think I am ignoring you."

"Something has happened in my family… something serious… and because of that, everyone in my house is disturbed."

"I can't tell you much right now, but I just want you to know that I am not avoiding you. It's just a bad time for me."

"I hope you understand."

"I will surely call you after a few days."

"And remember, as I told you earlier—I will never leave you at any cost."

- Munmun

I read the letter once.

Then twice.

And then five more times.

Every word, every line, every pause—I analysed them like a scientist conducting an experiment.

Confusion, Again

"I will never leave you at any cost."

Again, a confusing sentence.

Was it a promise?

Or just a friendly reassurance?

Did she love me?

Or was she just being a good friend?

This was the problem with girls.

They had this magical power to say things in a way that kept boys hanging between hope and heartbreak.

If a boy said, "I will never leave you at any cost," it meant just one thing—he was in love.

But when a girl said it, it could mean a hundred or even thousand different things.

And now, instead of feeling relieved, I was drowning in a new sea of overthinking.

The Overthinking Begins

"Something serious happened in my family…"

What did she mean by that?

Was it financial trouble?

Did someone in her family fall sick?

Or…

Did her father find out about me?

My heart skipped a beat.

I had heard stories—strict fathers, angry brothers, and scary family reactions when they found out their daughter was talking to a boy outside her caste.

And I remembered something Munmun once told me—

Her father had a pair of swords in their house.

Swords.

Not one, but two.

I imagined him sharpening them, preparing for an "inter-caste" execution.

Was he angry at her?

Was she being forced to stay away from me?

Was her brother involved?

A thousand questions flooded my mind, but I had zero answers.

And the worst part?

I had no way of finding out.

She had clearly said, "I will call you after a few days."

Which meant I had to wait.

But waiting was not my best skill.

Exams vs. Emotions

I had my Chemistry exam the day after tomorrow.

A subject that required focus, patience, and intense revision.

But my mind was now occupied with a subject called Munmun.

- I tried reading about Hydrocarbons, but all I could think of was "What happened in her house?"
- I tried memorizing the Periodic Table, but my brain replaced C for Carbon with C for Confusion.
- I tried solving numerical problems, but all I could calculate was the probability of Munmun's father knowing about me.

Hours passed, and I barely studied anything.

And for the first time in my life, I felt powerless.

Because this wasn't a math problem I could solve.

This wasn't a science experiment I could analyze.

This was life.

And in life, there are no formulas, no fixed answers—only uncertainty.

The Never-Ending Wait

Finally, exams were over.

For other students, it was a time to relax, to celebrate the end of school life.

But for me, nothing changed.

Because the one thing that mattered—her reply—was still missing.

Days passed.

My phone remained silent.

And I kept checking it every hour, every minute, waiting for her name to pop up on my screen.

But it never did.

And that's when I realized—

Sometimes, waiting is more painful than rejection.

Question for the readers
1. Have you ever felt torn between what you want and what others expect from you?
2. Do you believe in destiny? Or you are logical enough about the choices you make?

Chapter 14: The Worst Day

There are some days in life that change everything. Days that don't just hurt—they break you. July 17, 2018, was that day for me. The day when I lost something I never even truly had.

The Dream of a Better Future

I had always been a boy who followed rules. The obedient son. The sincere student. The one who never let distractions come in the way of his future.

After finishing my 12th boards, I joined computer classes to prepare myself for a better life. This time, I had promised myself—I would never go to a B-grade college again. No compromises. If I had to study, it would be at the best place—Patna University.

Unlike school, where marks decided everything, Patna University had only one requirement—an entrance exam. And I was ready for it.

I thought that was the only battle I had to fight. I had no idea that something far worse was coming my way.

The Call That Changed Everything

It was 5:30 PM, and I was walking back home from my computer institute. The evening air was warm, the streets were crowded, but my mind was lost in thoughts about my preparation.

Then, my phone rang.

I pulled it out of my pocket and froze.

"Munmun Calling…"

For a second, my heart skipped a beat. Why was she calling me?

Munmun never called randomly. If she ever did, she would always inform me beforehand. A strange feeling settled in my stomach—a feeling of unease.

I picked up the call.

"Hello?"

But the voice that answered wasn't hers.

"Who the hell are you?"

The voice was deep, rough, and filled with aggression. A chill ran down my spine.

"I… I am Romi," I said hesitantly.

"Shut up!" he snapped. "Why the f*** are you texting my sister?"

My stomach dropped. It was her cousin.

My grip on the phone tightened. My mind started racing. How did he get my number? Why was he calling me? What does he know?

"Sir, she is my friend," I said, my voice weak.

"Friend?" He let out a dry, mocking laugh. "Do you think I'm a fool?"

I opened my mouth to speak, but he cut me off.

"Listen to me carefully. If I find you calling or texting her again…"

I felt my breath hitch.

"I will kill you. Understood?"

My hands went numb. My knees felt weak. My vision blurred.

Before I could say a word, the call disconnected.

I stood there, frozen, in the middle of the road. My chest felt tight. My pulse was pounding. I wanted to scream, but no sound came out.

The words echoed in my head.

"I will kill you."

I wasn't a tough guy. I wasn't a street-smart boy who knew how to fight. I was just a simple, middle-class boy who loved a girl. And now, I was being threatened for it.

The Second Blow – The One That Destroyed Me

Somehow, I managed to drag myself home. But my nightmare wasn't over yet.

As soon as I entered my room, my phone rang again.

Unknown Number.

A fresh wave of fear gripped me. I knew this wasn't over.

My hands shook as I picked up the call.

"Hello?"

This time, it was Munmun's father.

His voice wasn't loud. It was calm. But somehow, that made it even scarier.

"Romi."

I held my breath.

"I never thought a boy like you would do something like this."

My lips trembled. My body felt cold.

"Uncle, I—"

"Stop." His voice was sharp. "I don't want to hear anything. You have disrespected my trust. You have insulted my family. How dare you?"

Tears welled up in my eyes. My throat burned.

"I… I am sorry, Uncle," I choked out.

But before I could say more, the phone was snatched away.

A new voice.

Munmun's mother.

Her words weren't just harsh. They were knives.

"Romi, I thought you were a good boy."

I felt something inside me break.

"But you are nothing but a traitor."

That word. Traitor.

My chest tightened. My lips quivered.

"Why have you done this?" she continued. "Don't you know we are Rajputs? How could you even THINK about Munmun in this way?"

My heart was screaming, but my mouth was silent.

I wanted to say, "Aunty, I never did anything wrong. I never disrespected her. I only loved her. I only wanted to be there for her."

But no one was ready to listen.

I couldn't hold back anymore. Tears poured down my face.

"I am sorry, Aunty… I didn't mean to… I—"

The call disconnected.

The Night That Felt Like Death

I sat on my bed, my phone slipping from my fingers onto the floor. I was shaking.

Everything inside me was breaking.

I wanted to scream, but what was the point?

I wanted to run, but where would I go?

I wanted to fix everything, but some things can never be fixed.

My dreams… my feelings… my love for Munmun… everything had been crushed in minutes.

I was not a criminal.

I was not a bad person.

I was not a traitor.

I was just a boy who fell in love.

But the world had decided that even that was a crime.

I buried my face in my hands and cried like a child.

For the first time in my life, I wished I could erase everything.

I wished I had never met Munmun.

I wished I had never fallen for her smile.

Because now, it was all over.

And the worst part?

I never even got to say goodbye.

Question for the readers

1. How do you move on when the people you love the most are the ones who break you the hardest?

2. What is your opinion about this situation in the story? Had Romi really made such a big mistake that he had to listen to this much?

Chapter 15: A Word from Munmun's Father

Some wounds are not of the body but of the heart. They don't bleed, yet they ache in ways no medicine can heal.

I am a father. My daughter, my Munmun, is my pride, my joy, and the very reason I have worked tirelessly all these years. Like every father, I have only one dream—to see my daughter safe, happy, and protected from the world's deceit.

And in this very world, there was a boy named Romi—a boy I once respected.

The First Meeting – A Father's Trust

I still remember the first time I met Romi. He was unlike most boys his age—soft-spoken, disciplined, and focused on his studies. He wasn't the kind who wasted his time on useless things. There was a sharpness in his eyes, the kind that only sincere students have.

I had heard his name before. He was a topper. People spoke well of him. My daughter mentioned him once or twice, always in a casual manner—"Papa, he's just a classmate."

I thought, Good. These are the kind of boys who inspire others to study, to stay away from bad habits.

Somewhere in my heart, I had grown fond of him. I would sometimes tell Munmun, "Keep good friends like Romi. See how hardworking he is?"

But life has a way of showing you that not everything is as it seems.

The Message That Changed Everything

That evening, I was sitting in the living room when Munmun's phone restarted due to some issue. As it switched back on, the backed-up messages started appearing one by one.

And then, I saw it.

A simple message.

"I like you, Munmun."

My hands froze.

My mind refused to believe what I was seeing. Romi? The same Romi I had respected?

A storm of emotions rose inside me. Disappointment. Shock. Betrayal.

It wasn't just about a boy liking my daughter. It was about trust.

I had seen Romi as a decent boy. I had trusted that he was different. And yet, here he was, crossing a boundary he should never have dared to.

For a long moment, I just stared at the screen. My hands clenched into fists. A father's instinct is always to protect, and in that moment, I felt like my trust had been violated.

I turned to Munmun, my voice firm yet controlled.

"What is this?"

She looked down. She had no answer.

That silence hurt me more than any words ever could.

A Father's Love, A Father's Pain

People say a father is always stricter than a mother. Maybe that's true. But behind that strictness is love deeper than the ocean.

Munmun is my only daughter. I have raised her with my principles, my values, and my protection. She is not just my child—she is my honor.

And Romi… he didn't just confess his feelings in a text.

He broke my trust.

Had he come to me, spoken to me with respect, maybe things would have been different. But this? This secrecy? This silent betrayal?

No. I could not let this happen.

Not because I hate Romi.

Not because I think he is a bad boy.

But because he forgot that love is not just about emotions. It is about respect. And he didn't respect the trust I had in him.

No Hatred, Only Disappointment

I hold no grudge against Romi's family. They are simple, hardworking people. I know his father is a waiter, his mother a housewife. They are good people. I do not look down upon them.

And I do not even hate Romi.

But I cannot forgive him either.

He had his whole life ahead of him—a bright future, a promising career. Why did he have to bring emotions into it? Why did he have to involve my daughter in his teenage dreams?

A Lesson for Every Boy

Love at this age? It is nothing but a distraction.

I have seen the world. I know what happens when a boy loses himself in emotions at the cost of his future. I have seen families torn apart, dreams shattered, and innocent love turning into regret.

I do not doubt that Romi's feelings were real. But a father does not think with emotions. He thinks with experience.

I had to stop this before it went any further. Because a father's greatest fear is not losing his daughter—it is losing her to a mistake she never should have made.

And so, I picked up the phone.

I dialled his number.

I listened to his trembling voice as I spoke, my words heavy, deliberate.

"I never thought a boy like you would do something like this, Romi."

And with that one sentence, I knew I had shattered him.

Maybe somewhere in another life, in another time, things could have been different. But not here. Not in this world.

Because here, in this world, a father's love always comes before a boy's affection.

Chapter 16: A Word from Munmun's Mother

A mother's heart is a strange thing. It is filled with endless love, yet it holds a strictness that even she does not enjoy. It knows how to forgive, yet it cannot forget.

I am a mother. My only daughter, Munmun, is my world. She is the light of my life, the dream I have woven with my own hands. And like every mother, I have spent my entire life making sure she walks on the right path, away from distractions, away from mistakes.

And then there was Romi—a boy I once thought was different.

The First Meeting – A Mother's Instinct

The first time I met Romi, I found him to be a nice boy. He was not like the others, who spoke too much, laughed too loudly, or carried arrogance in their eyes. He was soft-spoken, well-mannered, and deeply engrossed in his studies.

When I saw him, I thought, "This boy has been raised well."

He reminded me of the boys we used to admire in our time—the ones who respected elders, kept their heads down, and focused on making something of their lives.

There was nothing about Romi that would make me think he could ever do something wrong.

He wasn't someone who wasted time roaming around with friends, and he certainly didn't seem like the kind of boy who would make foolish mistakes when it came to girls.

I had met many of Munmun's friends before—some loud, some mischievous, some too modern for my liking. But Romi was different.

"He is a good boy," I had thought.

And I had believed it.

So, when Munmun mentioned his name once or twice in casual conversation, I never felt the need to question her.

"He's just a friend, Mummy," she would say.

And I trusted her.

I trusted him.

The Moment of Betrayal

Trust is such a fragile thing, isn't it? It takes years to build, but a single moment to shatter.

The day my husband found that message on Munmun's phone, I felt something inside me break.

"I like you, Munmun."

Just four words.

But in those four words, I saw the end of everything I had believed about Romi.

I felt betrayed.

I had trusted this boy, thought of him as someone good, someone different from the rest.

But he was just like them.

How could I have been so blind?

I felt a sharp pain in my heart, not just because of what Romi had done, but because of what it meant for Munmun.

Did she know? Did she feel the same way?

Or had she been hiding this from us all along?

I looked at my husband's face. His anger was not just anger—it was disappointment, heartbreak.

I could see it in his eyes.

For a father, the idea of his daughter being involved with a boy—even in the simplest, most innocent way—is enough to send his blood boiling.

And for a mother…

For a mother, it is fear.

Not anger. Not even disappointment.

Just pure, uncontrollable fear.

A fear that her daughter might be making a mistake. A fear that her world, so carefully built, could crumble in an instant.

A fear that everything she had worked so hard for—her dreams, her studies, her ambitions—would be reduced to just a boy's feelings.

The Call That Broke Me

I did not want to talk to Romi.

I did not want to hear his excuses, his justifications.

But when my husband handed me the phone, I knew I had to speak.

I had to let him know what he had done.

"Why, Romi?" I asked. My voice was not just angry—it was wounded.

"I thought you were a good boy. I thought you were different. But you… you are a traitor."

I heard him gasp.

He tried to say something, but his voice was trembling.

"Aunty… I never wanted to hurt you. I swear, I—"

"Hurt me?" I interrupted. "You have hurt yourself, Romi! You have hurt your own dignity! How could you do this?"

I could hear him crying on the other side.

And yet, my heart did not soften.

Because I was not just speaking as Romi's well-wisher that night.

I was speaking as a mother.

"Don't you know we are Rajputs?" I said, my voice shaking. "How could you even think of this? How could you even imagine my daughter this way?"

There was no reply.

Just silence.

And then, before I could say anything else, I cut the call.

I did not cry that night.

But I did not sleep either.

Because even after everything I had said, even after all the anger I had poured into that phone call, a part of me felt wrong.

A Mother's Protection

People say a mother's love is unconditional. But what they don't understand is that a mother's fear is just as deep as her love.

I did not hate Romi.

No.

I could not hate him.

Because in my heart, I knew he was not a bad boy.

But I also knew my daughter.

She was young. Innocent.

She had dreams of her own, ambitions that I wanted to see fulfilled.

And I knew how easily feelings could destroy all of that.

"A girl should dream, not just of love, but of success, of standing on her own feet, of making her parents proud."

That was what I had always believed.

That was what I had taught Munmun since she was a child.

And that was what I would continue to teach her, no matter what.

Maybe Romi's feelings were real. Maybe they were innocent.

But they had no place in Munmun's life.

Not now.

Not when she still had so far to go.

Maybe in another time, another life, things could have been different.

But in this life, my daughter had only one duty—to herself, to her family, and to her future.

And I would not let anything come in the way of that.

Not even a boy like Romi.

The Call I Made Later

Days passed. My anger faded, but my heart remained restless.

I kept thinking of Romi's voice that night. The way he broke down. The way he kept apologizing.

And so, one evening, I picked up the phone and called him again.

He hesitated before answering.

"Aunty…" his voice was weak, scared.

I took a deep breath.

"Romi… whatever I said that night… I said it in anger."

He remained silent.

"I do not hate you, beta. But you must understand… you cheated us. You broke our trust."

I heard his breathing grow heavy.

"I never wanted to hurt you, Aunty," he whispered.

"I know," I replied. "But some things are bigger than just feelings, Romi. Some things are about honor, about responsibility."

I could not say more.

I did not want to hurt him again.

And so, I ended the call.

But even after I put the phone down, my heart remained heavy.

Because I knew…

A mother's love is not just for her own child. It is for every child who has a pure heart.

And Romi… Romi was one of those children.

But he had chosen the wrong time, the wrong way.

And for that, I could not forgive him.

Question for the readers
1. Have you ever seen this kind of situation (till now in the story) from your parent's perspective?
2. Do you not think that Munmun's parents were right in this matter? If yes, Do you think Romi has done something wrong?

Chapter 17: The Sleepless Nights

They say time heals everything, but what if time itself stands still? What if every moment feels stretched, like a never-ending night, where sleep is just a forgotten luxury and peace is a distant dream?

Ever since that dreadful call, I had become a prisoner of my own thoughts. Fear gripped me like a shadow that refused to leave, following me in every waking moment. The moment I heard Munmun's cousin's voice on the phone, threatening me, warning me, something inside me broke. And when her father spoke—his voice laced with disappointment and anger—it shattered whatever was left of me.

Since that day, I had been living in constant anxiety. Every time my phone rang, I would freeze, my heart pounding so violently that I could hear it in my ears. I would stare at the screen, my fingers trembling over the answer button, my mind racing with a hundred terrifying possibilities. What if it was her father again? What if it was her brother, this time angrier than before? What if they weren't done with me yet?

I started avoiding unknown numbers. It was easier to live in uncertainty than to face another storm. But even then, the fear didn't leave me. It was inside me, poisoning my thoughts, making me second-guess every little thing.

I wanted to talk to someone—anyone—but who could I go to? My parents? No, never. Telling them meant destroying the image they had of me—their obedient, sincere son who had always made them proud. I imagined my father's face, the disbelief in his eyes when he would find out that his son had been warned by another man's family to stay away from their daughter. I imagined my mother's silence, the way she would simply lower her gaze, ashamed, disappointed. I couldn't let that happen.

So, I swallowed it all—the pain, the fear, the helplessness.

I pretended everything was normal. I ate with my family, nodding along to their conversations, though I barely heard a word. I sat with my books, staring at the pages, unable to read a single line. I went to sleep, only to spend the night tossing and turning, my eyes wide open, staring at the darkness, haunted by memories I wished I could erase.

And then came the loneliness—the kind that settles deep inside your bones, making you feel like a stranger in your own world. I had lost my connection with everyone. My friends, my classmates, even Shaima—I kept my distance from them all. How could I explain what I was going through? Who would understand?

I stopped using social media. I deactivated my accounts. WhatsApp, Facebook, Instagram—gone. I didn't want to see anyone, hear from anyone. I didn't want to risk stumbling upon Munmun's profile, seeing her living her life like nothing had happened, like I had never existed.

The worst part? I couldn't even blame her.

Maybe she was suffering too. Maybe she was feeling the same emptiness, the same weight on her chest. Or maybe... maybe she had moved on, and I was the only one still stuck in this misery.

A month passed.

Thirty days of torment. Thirty nights of sleeplessness.

And just when I had started to believe that the storm had settled, my phone rang again.

An unknown number.

I froze.

My fingers hovered over the screen. A battle raged inside me. Pick it up? Ignore it?

For a month, I had avoided unknown calls. But this time... this time, something told me I needed to answer.

I took a deep breath and swiped to accept.

"Hello?" I whispered.

There was silence for a moment. And then, a voice I recognized.

"Romii, it's me... Munmun's mother."

My breath caught in my throat.

For a moment, the world around me blurred. It was her. The same woman who had called me a traitor. The same woman who had humiliated me, questioned my worth, reminded me of the barriers that stood between me and her daughter.

I didn't know what to say. My heart pounded as I waited for her to continue.

She sighed. "I just wanted to say... whatever I told you that day... it was in anger."

I swallowed hard.

She hesitated before adding, "It wasn't from the heart."

A lump formed in my throat. My lips parted, but no words came out.

"But Romii..." Her voice softened, but it still carried the weight of disappointment. "You still did something wrong."

I blinked back the burning in my eyes. "I—I'm sorry, Aunty..."

"You don't need to apologize to me," she interrupted. "But think about what you've done to yourself in the past month. You've hurt yourself."

Hurt myself?

She was right.

I had lost myself in this pain. I had let their words consume me. I had turned into a shadow of the person I once was.

Before I could say anything, she disconnected the call.

And just like that, the silence returned.

But this time, it was different.

Because her words refused to leave my mind.

That night, I didn't sleep. But it wasn't because of fear. It was because I finally saw the truth.

I had let this pain define me.

I had let my feelings become my punishment.

But why? Was loving someone really such a terrible crime?

Tears slid down my face, silent and unending. For the first time in a month, I allowed myself to grieve. Not just for the love I lost, but for the person I had become.

But even in that darkness, there was a flicker of light.

The next morning, something changed. I looked at my books and, for the first time in weeks, I opened them. I forced myself to read, to write, to focus. It was hard, but I pushed through.

And then, days later, something unbelievable happened.

I checked my results.

I had qualified for Patna University.

Even after everything, even after losing myself for an entire month, I had still made it.

As I stood in front of the grand gates of Patna University, a strange emotion filled my chest.

Hope.

Maybe this was my second chance. Maybe I could start over. Maybe, just maybe, I could still become the person I was meant to be.

I wiped the last tear from my face.

Then, with a deep breath, I stepped forward.

It was time to begin again.

Chapter 18:
A Word from Romii's Mother

The day Romii was born, my world changed forever. I still remember that moment in the hospital—the soft cries of my baby, the warmth of his tiny fingers wrapping around mine. My heart swelled with a love so deep, so powerful, that I knew I would spend my entire life protecting him. He was not just my son; he was a part of my soul.

From that day, my only dream was to see him happy, safe, and successful. I called him my "chhota rajkumar", my little prince, and I meant it. He was the light in our small home, the joy in our simple lives.

Romii was never like other children. Where most kids ran around in the streets, got into fights, and played until their mothers dragged them home, Romii sat quietly with his books. He never demanded toys, never threw tantrums, never asked for expensive things. If I ever bought him a toy, he would play with it for a while, smile at me sweetly, and then go back to his studies. His world was small—just us, his books, and his dreams.

I had always told him, "Beta, padhai pe dhyaan do. Yeh duniya acchhe se acchhon ko neecha dikhane ka mauka dhoondti hai." And Romii listened. He listened so well that studies became his entire world.

I wanted to protect him. From bad company. From distractions. From anything that could take him away from his path. I never let him wander much outside, never let him waste time with unnecessary friendships. I thought I was doing the right thing, but today, when I look back...

Did I make a mistake?

I shaped him into a brilliant student, but in doing so, I stole his childhood. I kept him so focused on his books that he never learned how to express himself. I never encouraged him to explore the world beyond academics. And because of this, my son became an introvert.

His father always told him, "Beta, hamari family gareeb hai. Tujhe hi hamari taqdeer badalni hai." These words became his truth. He carried this weight on his small shoulders, believing that any distraction—any mistake— would mean he had failed us.

And that's why he never told us anything. Not about his dreams. Not about his struggles. Not about his heart.

I still remember the day he passed his 12th exams. He had scored so well, yet something in him had changed. He wasn't the same Romii anymore. He looked lost, his eyes carried a tiredness I couldn't understand.

I asked him so many times, "Beta, sab thik hai na?"

And every single time, he just smiled and said, "Haan, Maa. Sab thik hai."

But I knew... everything was not fine.

I saw how he stared at his phone, lost in thoughts. How he avoided conversations, how his laughter became rare, how his shoulders carried an invisible burden. I saw it all, but he never told me.

And now, as I look back, I realize—maybe he thought we wouldn't understand. Maybe he thought we would scold him, that we would see him as weak.

But he was wrong.

I am his mother. Before anyone else, I would have understood him. I regret not telling him more often that he could talk to me about anything. I regret making him believe that his worth was only in his studies. I regret that he suffered alone when he didn't have to.

But despite all this, I am proud of my son.

He may not have shared everything with us, but he never let his struggles define him. He carried his responsibilities with grace. He fought his battles silently, without asking for help. He sacrificed his childhood for our dreams, and yet, he never complained.

And today, as I see him stepping into Patna University, I know—he has become a man.

Maybe I made mistakes as a mother. Maybe I should have let him be a child a little longer. But one thing is certain—

Romii is not just a good student.

He is one of the best sons a mother could ever ask for from god.

Question for the readers

1. Why is it so difficult for teenagers in most of the Indian families to discuss these emotions with their parents?
2. Do Indian families see these feelings as a social taboo? If yes, who are responsible for this?

Chapter 19: The Realisation

One year had passed.

Three hundred and sixty-five days since that call, since that evening when my world flipped upside down. I had thought time would make things easier, that with each passing day, the memories would fade, and my heart would grow lighter. But the truth was different—time didn't erase anything. It only helped me understand the weight of what had happened.

Looking back, I still couldn't say I had done something terribly wrong. Having feelings for someone isn't a crime. Loving someone, admiring them, wanting to be a part of their world—these are all natural emotions. I wasn't guilty of any wrongdoing. But I was guilty of something else—I had broken the trust of people who once believed in me.

Munmun's father, who had once seen a bright future in me.

Munmun's mother, who had thought of me as a gentle and well-mannered boy.

And maybe, even Munmun herself.

That trust wasn't just lost—it was shattered. And no matter how much I wished to go back and undo everything, life doesn't work that way.

Munmun still occupied my thoughts, and I couldn't fight it. Every morning, her face would flash in my mind before I could even stop myself. Every little thing reminded me of her—the streets we had walked together, the jokes we had laughed at, the way she smiled when she talked about silly things. She was the first person who had ever made me feel important.

And maybe, that was the hardest part.

People talk about "moving on" as if it's a simple formula—just find a distraction, meet new people, bury yourself in work, and one day, you'll wake up without the pain. But that never happened for me.

I had joined Patna University. A new place, a fresh start. I had taken literature as my core subject, along with history and political science. Books and words had become my escape, but even within the pages of poetry and prose, I found her.

One whole year had passed, and still, I hadn't moved on.

The world expected me to. Society expected me to. Because apparently, boys aren't supposed to hold on to emotions for too long.

But that's when I realized something important—moving on is not a rule. It's not a universal truth that applies to everyone.

It's subjective. For some, it takes days. For others, weeks or months. And for some, like me, it just never truly happens.

And that doesn't make me weak.

It just makes me human.

Society always paint boys as the ones who "move on quickly," who "don't get too attached," who "forget and move forward without looking back." But why is it so hard for people to believe that boys feel deeply too?

I was proof that we do. That sometimes, even after a year, even after life moves forward, a part of us remains stuck in the past.

I had met many people in the past year. New classmates, new friends, even girls who were interested in talking to me. But no matter how much I tried, I couldn't find that same spark, that same feeling that I had with Munmun. It wasn't about her being the most beautiful girl, or the smartest. It was about the way she made me feel. The way she made me believe that I was worth something.

Maybe that's why some people never truly move on—because some emotions aren't meant to be replaced.

Science says that the human brain craves closure. That we seek logical endings to the chapters of our lives. But what if closure isn't always possible?

What if, instead of closing the chapter, we just learn to live with the story?

That's what I had started doing—learning to live with the memories, without letting them break me. I was not a victim of love. I was just a boy who had loved, lost, and learned.

And maybe, just maybe, some feelings are meant to stay—not as wounds, but as reminders that once in this lifetime, we felt something real.

Question for the readers

1. In your opinion, what would be the correct age of a teenager like Romi to understand that the career is way more important than a mere crush? Were you intelligent enough at that age to understand these things deeply?

2. Is "moving on" even a concept or humans have just made the term popular for their convenience?

Chapter 20: Career Comes First

Some lessons in life come late. Some realizations only arrive after you've lost something, after you've wandered through sleepless nights, after you've fought battles within yourself that no one else can see.

If I had understood earlier that love and career are two different paths that should never be mixed, maybe my journey would have been different. Maybe I would have achieved things much sooner, saved myself from unnecessary pain, and focused on what truly mattered. But life doesn't give wisdom without experience. You can't learn a lesson unless you feel it deep inside you. And I—like everyone else—had to learn it the hard way.

Today, I stand at a different point in my life. A place where I have clarity, where I understand why things happened the way they did. And for the first time, I don't feel regret.

The Journey of Dreams and Distractions

When I was younger, my dreams were simple. I wanted to study hard, secure a stable future, and make my parents proud. My father, who spent his life serving food to others, always told me, "Beta, humare naseeb ki zindagi mat jeena. Tumhare haathon mein kalam achha lagta hai, tray nahi." (Son, don't live a life like ours. A pen suits your hands, not a serving tray.) His words became my mission. I knew I had no choice but to succeed.

And for the most part, I was doing exactly that. Until the so called love entered into my life.

She came into my life like a soft breeze, unexpected yet comforting. She made me laugh, made me feel seen. For the first time, I wasn't just a 'topper' or a 'studious guy.' I was Romi, the boy who could make her smile. And that feeling was intoxicating.

But love has a way of clouding judgment. I was so caught up in emotions, in the magic of our little moments, that I never realized I was losing myself. I was still scoring well, still following my routine, but mentally, I had drifted. My focus wasn't just on my dreams anymore; it was on her—on her texts, her laughs, her existence in my life.

And then, just like that, she was gone.

Her father's call, her mother's scolding, the sudden erasure of her from my life—it all shattered me. I lost her, but more than that, I lost a part of myself. I stopped studying the way I used to. I stopped caring about my ambitions. My confidence broke, my mind became restless, and for months, I was trapped in a cycle of regret and pain.

The Awakening

One day, I looked at myself in the mirror and saw someone I didn't recognize. A boy who once had dreams, who once wanted to change his family's fate, was now drowning in thoughts of a girl who was never his.

And that's when it hit me—Munmun was never the destination. She was just a part of the journey.

I promised myself that day: No more distractions. No more regrets.

I shut everything else out and focused only on my studies. I worked harder than ever, not because I wanted to escape my past, but because I wanted to rebuild myself. I wanted to prove that I was not just a boy who loved a girl—I was a boy who had a purpose.

And that purpose led me to success.

The Day of Victory

After years of relentless hard work, I finally achieved what I had always dreamed of. I graduated. I cleared my exams. I got a government job.

The day I received my appointment letter, I saw tears in my mother's eyes and pride in my father's silent nod. This was their dream. This was what they had sacrificed their whole lives for. And at that moment, I realized—this victory was bigger than me.

My success wasn't just about getting a job. It was about changing the destiny of my family. It was about ensuring that my mother never had to worry about grocery bills, that my father never had to bow his head in front of anyone.

And that feeling—that sense of purpose—was far greater than any love I had ever known.

Does that mean I have forgotten Munmun? No.

She was, and will always be, a special part of my life. But now, she is not a wound—she is a lesson. A reminder that I was once capable of deep emotions. A reminder that love is beautiful, but it should never come at the cost of one's own future.

I still think about her sometimes. Not with sadness, not with bitterness, but with gratitude. She made me realize my worth. She made me stronger.

Today, when I look back at those days—when I see that boy who cracked lame jokes just to see her smile—I smile too. Not because I miss those days, but because I know now that happiness is not just found in love. It is found in purpose.

To Those Who Are Struggling

To anyone who is going through heartbreak, to those who feel lost, let me tell you one thing—your dreams deserve your undivided attention. Love will come and go, but your ambitions will shape your entire life.

Focus on yourself. Build yourself. Because one day, when you stand victorious, you will realize that everything you lost was only making way for something greater.

And on that day, like me, you will smile too.

Chapter 21: Rewind to the Past

Some moments in life feel like a dream, as if they belong to another lifetime. They become so distant that when we recall them, they don't feel like our own memories, but rather a story we once heard. This was one of those moments.

A Reunion After a Long Time

It was April 2023—one of those warm summer evenings in Patna when the setting sun painted the sky in hues of orange and gold. The city had changed, or maybe I had changed. The streets that once felt familiar now seemed like distant echoes of my past. Life had moved on, and so had I, but every now and then, the past had a strange way of sneaking up on me.

I was with Avikal and Amit, my old friends—the only ones who had been a part of my journey from the beginning. We hadn't met in a long time. College, career, and responsibilities had scattered us in different directions. But today, fate had brought us together again, and for a few hours, we sat there, laughing, reminiscing, and talking about life.

Avikal had secured a job in a multinational company as a junior developer. He spoke about his work with excitement in his eyes—about coding, deadlines, and the thrill of working in a fast-paced environment. He had always been ambitious, and seeing him achieve his dreams made me proud. Amit, on the other hand, had taken a different path, exploring business opportunities. Each of us had carved our own journeys, but sitting there, cracking jokes, it felt like nothing had changed. We were still the same boys who once roamed the streets of Patna, carefree and full of dreams.

As the conversation continued, I glanced at my watch. It was getting late. I had pending work at home, and my disciplined nature wouldn't let me sit idly for long. "Chalo bhai, mujhe nikalna hoga. Ghar pe kaam hai," I said, standing up.

Amit rolled his eyes. "Tu abhi bhi waise ka waisa hi hai, Romii. Ek minute extra rukna tere liye paap jaisa hai."

Avikal chuckled. "Arre rehne de, ab iska time table set hai. Ek second idhar-udhar ho gaya toh iska pura system crash ho jayega."

I laughed, shaking my head. They were right. I had changed. The boy who once wandered aimlessly, lost in emotions and overthinking, had now become someone who prioritized his time like a strict accountant. Maybe life had taught me that time waits for no one. Maybe I had learned that dwelling on the past does nothing but steal the present.

I waved them goodbye and walked out of the small gali onto the main road, unaware that life was about to give me an unexpected encounter.

A Face from the Past

As I stepped onto the bustling road, my eyes instinctively scanned the crowd, and then... I saw her.

Munmun.

For a second, time froze. The sounds of honking vehicles, the rush of people, the heat of the April evening—it all faded into the background. All that remained was her.

She was on a bike, sitting behind someone. I didn't know who he was, and surprisingly, I didn't even care to know. My eyes were on her. The girl who had once defined beauty for me. The girl whose smile had once made my heart race. The girl whose absence had left me in turmoil for months.

She looked just as radiant as I remembered. The same long, silky hair that once danced in the wind when I sat behind her on her scooty. The same deep, expressive eyes that had once made me feel special, like I was someone important. She had changed in some ways—maybe a little more mature, a little more grown—but the essence of Munmun remained the same.

A year ago, if I had seen this sight, my mind would have spiraled into a storm of thoughts. Who is he? Is he her boyfriend? How many boyfriends has she had after me? Does she still remember me? Does she ever think about me?

But today, as I stood there watching her disappear into the distance, not a single question crossed my mind.

Instead, a soft smile crept onto my lips.

The Beauty of Acceptance

For the first time, I wasn't overthinking. I wasn't feeling pain. I wasn't feeling jealousy. I wasn't feeling regret. I was just... at peace.

I realized something in that moment—we don't truly move on by forcing ourselves to forget someone, we move on when remembering them no longer hurts.

She was a part of my story. A beautiful, unforgettable part. But she was not my present, and she was not my future. She was a chapter that had been written in golden ink, but one that had ended long ago.

I still cherished the memories—the way I had struggled to make her laugh, the way I had felt nervous yet ecstatic sitting behind her on her scooty, the way my heart had raced when she gave me her number for the first time. Those moments were real, and they would always remain special.

But today, they were just memories. Nothing more, nothing less.

I turned away, took a deep breath, and continued walking. The past was behind me, and the future was waiting ahead.

Whoever said that a boy's capacity to love and express emotions decreases with age was right. As we grow, our emotions don't vanish, but they evolve. Love, heartbreak, longing—they all become different. We stop overthinking. We stop expecting. We learn to let go, not because we stop caring, but because we learn that life never stops moving forward.

As I walked home that evening, I didn't feel sad. I didn't feel lost. I just felt grateful. Grateful for the lessons, for the emotions, for the pain, for the growth.

And most of all, grateful for the realization that I was finally free.

Chapter 22: A Message for the Youngsters

Life is a teacher. It doesn't give lessons in a classroom, nor does it come with a syllabus. It teaches through experiences—some bitter, some sweet, but all important. Looking back at my journey, I realize how much I have grown, how much I have learned, and how much I wish I had understood earlier.

This chapter is not just my story; it's a message to all the young students, especially those who are standing at the crossroads of emotions and responsibilities. If you are reading this, I want you to know that I was once like you—a boy with dreams, a heart full of emotions, and a mind filled with distractions. I made mistakes, I suffered, I learned. And today, I want to share those lessons with you.

1. Love is Not a Distraction, but It Can Become One

Let's be honest—having feelings for someone is not wrong. In fact, it's one of the most beautiful emotions that life has to offer. But there's a time and place for everything. When you are a student, your primary focus should be on building your future. Love is not a distraction in itself, but when it begins to consume your mind, affect your studies, and take away your peace, it becomes one.

I learned this the hard way. When I met Munmun, she became the center of my world. My focus shifted from books to messages, from dreams to daydreams. And when things went wrong, I was left shattered. I lost precious time overthinking, grieving, and isolating myself. Had I realized earlier that emotions should be handled with balance, I wouldn't have suffered so much.

So, my advice is simple: if you have feelings for someone, don't let them overpower your purpose. If it's meant to be, it will find its way at the right time. But right now, your priority should be yourself and your career.

2. Your Career Should Be Your First Love

One harsh reality of life is that emotions are temporary, but your career is permanent. The person you are thinking about today may not even be a part of your life tomorrow. But the skills and knowledge you gain today will stay with you forever.

Had I focused more on my studies rather than drowning in emotions, I could have achieved much more, much earlier. But I don't regret it, because every experience teaches something. Now, I understand that no matter what happens in life, a strong career will always be my biggest strength.

Youngsters often get swayed by emotions and neglect their future. But remember this—one day, you will realize that success and financial stability give a different kind of confidence, one that no relationship can provide.

3. Time is the Most Precious Asset

If there is one thing that never comes back, it is time. The hours you spend stalking someone's social media, overthinking about the past, or waiting for someone's reply—none of that will add any value to your life. But the same time, if invested in learning, reading, or improving yourself, will change your life forever.

I wasted so many nights staring at my phone, waiting for a message that never came, drowning in thoughts that only pulled me down. And for what? Did it change anything? No. It only made me lose focus, made me weaker, and stole my peace.

So, I urge every youngster reading this—use your time wisely. Don't spend it chasing people who may not even care. Instead, invest it in something that will make your future brighter.

4. Overthinking is Your Biggest Enemy

I used to overthink everything—Does she still think about me? Does she regret leaving me? Did I do something wrong? These thoughts played in my mind like a broken record, and no matter how much I tried, they wouldn't stop.

But one day, I realized a simple truth: Thinking too much about something doesn't change the reality. It only makes you suffer more.

So, if you find yourself overthinking about someone or something, stop. Train your mind to let go. Learn to focus on what you can control, and leave the rest.

Overthinking will only drain your energy and make you miss out on the present.

5. Self-Respect Over Everything

One of the biggest mistakes youngsters make is begging for attention and love. We lose our self-respect in the process of making someone else happy. I, too, made that mistake. I kept waiting for a message, an apology, a sign that she still cared. But in the end, all I got was disappointment.

Self-respect means knowing your worth. If someone values you, they will make an effort. If they don't, then you should have the courage to walk away. Never let anyone make you feel like you are not enough.

6. Pain is Temporary, But Lessons are Forever

Heartbreak feels like the end of the world, but trust me, it's not. The pain you feel today will fade tomorrow, but the lesson it teaches you will stay for life.

I used to think I would never move on, that the pain would never end. But today, I smile when I think about the past. Not because I don't remember the pain, but because I have grown from it.

If you are going through a tough time, know that it will pass. Time heals, and one day, you will look back and realize that everything happened for a reason.

7. You Are Your Own Priority

In the end, the only person who will stay with you forever is you. People will come and go, but your relationship with yourself is the most important one. So, take care of yourself. Work on yourself. Grow, learn, and become the best version of yourself.

When I started prioritizing myself, everything changed. I became stronger, more confident, and happier. And you can too.

Final Words

To every young reader who is reading this, remember:

- Love is beautiful, but don't let it distract you.
- Your career should be your top priority.
- Time is precious—don't waste it on things that don't matter.
- Overthinking will only hurt you.
- Self-respect is more important than temporary happiness.
- Pain will pass, but lessons will stay.
- Most importantly, you are your biggest asset—invest in yourself.

Life is long, and you have so much to achieve. Don't let temporary emotions hold you back from building a future that you deserve.

I was once a boy who let his emotions dictate his life. But today, I have learned that true strength comes from balance. Love will come and go, but your dreams, your ambitions, and your self-worth should never take a backseat.

So, my dear young friends, focus on what truly matters. Build your life first, and everything else will fall into place at the right time.

Chapter 23: A Word from Avikal and Amit

(A vikal clears his throat)

"Arey bhai, kahani khatam hone wali hai aur hum dono ka mention tak nahi tha?"

(Amit nods)

"Bilkul! Romii ki story uske bestiess ke bina adhoori hai!"

Toh doston, hum hain Avikal aur Amit—Romii ke school-time wale purane dost. Matlab wahi waale jo sirf dosti nahi, bhai waale connection rakhte hain. Aur jab tak hum dono apni taraf se kuch na bol dein, tab tak ye kahani complete nahi hogi.

Avikal's Turn

Romii is not just any ordinary guy. He is that one friend who silently carries the weight of everything on his shoulders and still acts like nothing ever bothers him. If you meet him for the first time, you might think he is just a serious, career-oriented guy with no distractions. But trust me, that's just his outer shell. Deep inside, he is a person full of emotions, kindness, and, most importantly, the ability to suffer in silence.

I remember back in school—Romii was the topper. The teachers loved him, the students respected him, and we, his friends, just enjoyed calling him 'Babu Saheb' because, let's be honest, he had a royal attitude when it came to studies. No one dared to challenge him in exams, and honestly, we didn't even try. Who would compete with a walking, talking encyclopedia?

But the real twist in his life came when he met Munmun. And let me tell you, it was hilarious to see a guy like Romii, who always kept a safe distance from girls, suddenly start cracking lame jokes just to impress one. We knew something was up, but being the introvert that I am, I never asked him directly. I could see the changes in him—his sudden distraction, the way he would stare at his phone in between conversations, and the way his smile had a different glow. It was new for us to see Romii like this, but honestly, it was kind of nice.

Then came the phase where things went wrong. I don't know what exactly happened, but I knew he was hurting. Romii is the type of person who won't tell you he's upset, but you can see it in his silence. His laughter became less frequent, he started keeping to himself, and worst of all, he stopped cracking his terrible jokes—which, believe it or not, we actually missed.

I wanted to talk to him, but the problem was, I was also an introvert. We both shared that unspoken rule of "not talking about feelings." So, I just stayed beside him, hoping that my presence was enough to let him know that he wasn't alone.

(Amit)

Now, let me take over from here. Unlike Avikal, I am not an introvert. I believe in saying things as they are. And one thing I can say with full confidence is that Romii is one of the strongest people I know.

There was a time when I was going through a major financial crisis. I didn't tell anyone because, let's be honest, nobody likes to ask for help. But somehow, Romii found out. And without saying a single word, he transferred money into my account. When I asked him why, he just said, "Bhai, return it when you can. No pressure."

That moment made me realize something—Romii might not be the most expressive person, but he cares deeply. He doesn't show it in grand gestures, but in the small things he does. That's what makes him special.

People say that love changes a person, and I agree. But I also believe that heartbreak makes a person stronger. Romii is proof of that. He went through pain, he suffered in silence, but he never lost himself. Instead, he became wiser, more mature, and more focused.

If you ask me, I'd say Romii is the kind of person who may not say much, but his actions speak volumes. He has always been there for us, and I know he always will be.

(Avikal)

So, if you're wondering what kind of person Romii is, let me summarize it for you:

- He is a topper but never makes others feel less intelligent.
- He is responsible but also carries a childish innocence.
- He is introverted but cares more than anyone else.
- He is mentally strong but has a heart that feels deeply.

And most importantly, he is the kind of friend everyone wishes to have.

Amit and I have seen Romii at his best and at his worst. And through everything, one thing has remained constant—his loyalty, his kindness, and his ability to rise above any situation.

So, dear readers, you now have our perspective on Romii. The question is—how does your perspective about him change after reading all this?

Chapter 24: Shaima Again

"Hey readers, I hope you haven't forgotten me!"

(Yes, it's me—Shaima. Romii's sister, his confidante, and an important part of this story. This is my third appearance in the book, but I won't take much of your time. I just have something very important to say, something that perhaps no one has thought about yet.)

Throughout this book, you have seen everything from Romii's perspective—his emotions, his pain, his happiness, his love, and even his heartbreak. You have felt his struggles, his sleepless nights, and his journey of self-discovery.

But tell me one thing—what about Munmun?

Yes, Romii's love was true. His feelings were genuine. But do you really think Munmun never felt anything? Do you think she never had emotions of her own? Do you believe that she simply walked away without any second thoughts?

Love is experienced differently by boys and girls. A boy's world is often simple—if he likes someone, that person becomes the most special to him. If he falls in love, he imagines a future with that one person, without thinking much about complications. But for girls, emotions are layered, their thoughts deeper. They live in a world where their choices are influenced by family, society, and their own expectations.

I remember the day Romii came to me after writing the first draft of this book. He titled it "Munmun." I smiled and asked him, "But where is Munmun's story? Your readers deserve to know her side too."

And I know, deep down, even Romii wanted that.

So now, dear readers, let's turn the page and step into the perspective of Romii's first crush—the girl who unknowingly changed his life forever.

With that, I welcome you to Munmun's Story.

Question for the readers
1. Do you have a Shaima like cousin/friend in your life? If yes, let them know. If no, make one.

Chapter 25: A Word from Romii's First Crush, Munmun

"Pehchana mujhe?"

For the first time in this entire book, I, Munmun, am speaking to you all. Strange, isn't it? Reading a book about me, but hearing my side of the story only in the last chapter. But maybe this was necessary. Maybe this is how life works—sometimes, you hear only one side of the story for years before realizing there was another side, just as real, just as emotional.

I know this book is written from Romii's perspective, but I also know one thing—Romii will never paint me as a villain. Itni izzat to banti hai na? After all, I was his first crush. And maybe… just maybe, he was mine too.

The First Impression

I still remember the first time I noticed Romii in school. He was that quiet, studious boy who never got involved in unnecessary things. While most boys in our school were busy trying to show off, Romii was different. There was something about him—maybe his sincerity, maybe the way he was always lost in his books, or maybe the way he never sought attention yet always managed to stand out. I knew even back then that this boy would go a long way.

Then came our first real interaction in college. Honestly, I won't lie—I found him cute. Not in a childish way, but in a way that made me feel safe, like he was someone who wouldn't hurt anyone. And when we started talking, I started liking him—not the way he liked me, but in my own way.

Shaima was right—the definition of liking is different for boys and girls. For Romii, liking me meant wanting to be close to me, cherishing every moment, and maybe even dreaming about a future together. But for me, liking him meant admiring him, appreciating his presence, and feeling comfortable around him in a way I never felt with anyone else.

The Day Everything Changed

I know the day my brother and father called him and scolded him must have been one of the worst days of his life. And trust me, it wasn't easy for me either. That day, I felt something I had never felt before—guilt. But what could I have done? Ladka hoti to shayad kuch keh bhi deti, par ek ladki ke liye apni family ke against jaana itna asaan nahi hota.

I wanted to reach out. I wanted to tell him that I didn't hate him, that he wasn't wrong for expressing his feelings. But I remained silent. And that silence created a distance between us that could never be filled again.

Time passed, life moved on, and so did we.

Or did we?

Memories That Never Faded

Even after all these years, whenever I see Romii's pictures somewhere—on social media, in old college group photos, or even just in my memories—I smile. And not just any smile, but that smile. The same smile I had when we rode together on my scooty, the same smile I had when he cracked his lame but adorable jokes just to make me laugh.

Romii, I hope you still like my smile.

But you know what you forgot to mention in your book? That one day in college, you casually said, "Teri aankhein bohot sundar hain, par yeh chashma uss sundarta ko chhupa deta hai."

That day, I didn't say anything, but after that, I started looking at myself differently. Even today, after reading this book, I'll stand in front of the mirror, remove my glasses, and smile—just for you.

A Message for Romii

Romii, I know you think of me as the girl who changed your life. But the truth is, you changed mine too. You taught me what respect looks like, what it feels like to be genuinely valued. You showed me that not all boys look at a girl with just attraction—some look at her with admiration, with respect, with care.

And for that, I will always be grateful.

You have always been a tough guy, Romii. Stronger than you know. And today, like everyone else who has read this book, I am also proud of you.

Not as your crush.

Not as your past.

But as your friend.

Yours,

Munmun.

www.ingramcontent.com/pod-product-compliance
Lightning Source LLC
LaVergne TN
LVHW041607070526
838199LV00052B/3030